DEAD MAN'S GOLD

Vern sure had the knack of getting into a parcel of trouble. First the damfool cattle had stampeded, and he'd been sent to find and bring back the twenty-odd beefs that had gone and lost themselves. Then he discovered the dead Spaniard — with pockets full of gold! Dead man or not, gold was gold, and Vern was not about to let this opportunity pass him by. So he would hunt down the source of that lost gold mine, and that was the real beginning of his trouble. Because how far can a man get in rugged country without his horse, his gun and his boots . . . and with a mad old coot tracking him down!

DEAD MAN'S GOLD

LEE HOFFMAN

SAGEBRUSH
Large Print Westerns

First published in the United States by Ace Books

First Isis Edition
published 2021
by arrangement with
Golden West Literary Agency

A catalogue record for this book is available
from the British Library.

ISBN 978–1–78541–870–9

Published by
Ulverscroft Limited
Anstey, Leicestershire

Set by Words & Graphics Ltd.
Anstey, Leicestershire
Printed and bound in Great Britain by
TJ Books Ltd., Padstow, Cornwall

This book is printed on acid-free paper

CHAPTER
ONE

It was in a glade on the bottom slopes of Grizzly Mountain that they found the hat.

They'd left Medina as part of the crew trailing two thousand head, some of it she-stuff for a rancher name of Gil Nash up on the Home River, and the rest feeders going to winter on the long grass of Wyoming. It was in the valley along the foot of Old Grizzly that they bedded the herd one night, and everything had looked fine and peaceable until well after midnight. Then something decided the beefs to go for a run.

It wasn't a bad run. There'd been worse troubles down along the Pecos. When the cattle were settled again and the sky had turned light enough for the men to see what they had, they weren't more than three miles off the bed-ground. The beefs all looked fine and happy and ready for a long day of walking. But that ornery old golondrino steer that had been in the lead off to the right was missing, along with about twenty head of mixed steers and she-stuff.

The Boss said he kind of hoped they'd just gotten separated and gone for a walk in the brush on the low slopes of the mountain. He figured they were likely all bunched up together and resting from their run. At least he hoped so. The three hands he sent to look for them hoped so too. Their orders were to find the strays and catch them up to the herd, no *ifs* mentioned.

It was the kid, Snuffy, still riding his bay night horse, who came onto the hat. The horse stepped into it in the long grass. It hung up on his hoof, looking like an old rusty pot with a hole in it. The bay went up, four legs stiff, his spine bent in the middle till his rump was tucked under his chin. Snuffy grabbed the apple and gave out a holler.

The three of them had spread out to look for the strays but Pike and Vernon were still both within earshot. Snuffy's shout brought them dashing toward him. When they saw what was going on, they stopped to watch. It took them both a minute or two to realize that Snuffy was still young and green and too busy to appreciate the fun, so they gave a hand. Finally they got the bay calmed down enough for the kid to pull that contraption off its leg.

Snuffy dropped the thing and wiped at his face. Hunkering down, he said something about how the horse needed a little rest after all that commotion. From the way he leaned his back against a rock and hung his hands over his knees, it looked like it was he who needed the rest.

But the others didn't argue with him. They'd all ridden through the run that night and were feeling like they'd begin to take root to their saddles. Pike stretched a leg over the cantle and dropped off his horse with a grunt like an old bull. Then Vernon swung down too, walking stiff and weary. He bent from the knees,

2

hunkering to pick up that rusty old pot and turn it curiously in his hands.

"It's a hat," he said.

"Huh?" Snuff grunted.

"It's a tin bucket some emigrant lost," Pike said with a derisive snort. He looked at Vern as if he wondered what kind of weeds he'd been chawing.

"One of them old Spanish soldier hats," Vern told them. He tilted it up at an angle. "See here?"

"See if it fits you," Snuffy suggested.

Vern pulled off his sombrero and tried the hat over his shaggy tow thatch. It was too small.

"What would a Spanish soldier be doing up here?" Pike said skeptically. "Were a hell of a long ways from Mex."

"They came around here. All this country around here used to be Spanish back in the old days. Them Spanish explorers come through here looking for cities made out of gold and all such," Vern answered him.

"Book-learnin'," he muttered as if he didn't put much stock in such things.

But Snuffy looked real interested. "You reckon there's gold around here?"

"Might be," Vern mumbled, gazing up at the bare gray face of granite near the peak of Old Grizzly.

But Pike only dug at the dirt with the toe of his boot. He brought up about half of an airtight, the rest eaten away with rust. "There's your gold. And your Spaniard, too. Did them Spanish explorers use airtights, Vern?"

"Not as I know of."

3

"Some emigrant's Spanish bucket," he said with satisfaction, as if his opinion had been undeniably vindicated.

Snuffy wasn't paying any attention. He seemed to have become fascinated by the bushes behind Vern. He leaned forward, dropping to all fours, and peered under them. The others watched with blank-eyed curiosity as he crept forward, not sure whether he'd flush a woodchuck or the old golondrino. But nothing fled from the brush and after a moment Snuffy backed out again.

He looked at them through wide eyes and said in a hushed voice, "Dead critter in there what ain't never been decent buried."

"What kind of critter?" Pike asked.

"*Man* critter."

This time they all stuck their heads into the thicket.

The skeleton was old and crumbling. It was mixed up, with leg bones, ribs and skull all confused. Only the shapes of the bones showed that it had once been human — those and the rusted remains of the Spanish breastplate that lay half-buried in the ground.

When Vern picked up a stick and prodded at the plate, it broke into pieces, showing them a chunk of backbone with a small bit of gray stone — an arrowhead — lodged into it.

"Whoowee!" Snuffy said. "Look at that!"

"Injuns. Got the poor old devil good," Vern muttered.

"You reckon they're still around here?" Snuffy asked, swinging his head to scan the countryside warily.

"No. Not the same bunch, they ain't." Vern poked the arrowhead with his stick until it jarred loose from

4

the decaying bone. Then he dragged at it until he could pick it up without reaching into the bone heap. Turning it between his fingers, he said, "Real nice piece of work. Got a good edge on it. Injuns don't make 'em out'n stone like that no more."

"Something else here, too." Snuff picked up a broken branch and began to work at a lump in the ground. It seemed to have a bit of root or vine sticking up from it. Or maybe it was an old dried-up leather string. The stick pried and it came up from under the dirt, falling apart and spilling shards of rock on the ground. The rock was white. The streaks and splotches of yellow in it were shiny bright.

Deep in his throat, Pike said, "Gold!"

He thrust his hand in, heedless of the dead man, and grabbed his fingers full of the shards. Looking close, he repeated, "Gold!"

"Fools' gold," Vern suggested uncertainly.

Pike shook his head.

"From around *here*?" Snuff squinted at the veined quartz ore, then looked up at the granite-faced peak.

"From out *his* poke," Vern said, nodding toward the bones. He pushed his stick at the earthy lump that had spilled the gold. It stirred the rotted remains of a leather pouch. "That money sack weathered better'n he did."

"This here is raw ore, straight out the ground," Pike told them.

"Out *his* poke," Vern repeated.

"Then *he* got it straight out the ground," Pike insisted.

5

"Where you reckon he was coming from with it?" Snuffy asked, still staling upward.

Vern studied the earth under the bush. There was a lot of broken stone mixed in with the dirt. He looked toward the slope rising sharply above them. "I think the land fell away from up there. Long time ago. Long enough for this old feller to get growed over with bushes."

He pointed in the direction he gazed, toward a ledge overgrown with trees. There was a gap in its edge, grooving down its face. There were a few speckles of brush growing in it, but for the most part it was bare, cut straight down the mountainside like a dried-up water run.

"See there." He waggled his aimed finger. "That gully yonder?"

Snuffy nodded.

"Way I'd figure it, this old Spaniard was lying dead up there a while. Then the ground washed out from under him and he tumbled down here, along with all this busted up rock."

"Let's go up and take a look around," Snuffy suggested. Pike bobbed his head in violent agreement.

But Vern snorted, "We got to find them strays and catch up to the herd right quick or we'll miss chuck."

"Chuck! You're worried about food!" Pike was almost hollering with excitement. "Hell, man! We got enough gold right here to set us all to one hell of a feed up to Cheyenne. If we go look around up there, mebbe we'll find more!"

6

"Hell's what the Boss'll give us if we don't fetch them beefs back real soon," Vern muttered, gazing at the gold in Pike's hand. He could have reached out and touched it, but yet somehow it didn't seem real. Quick riches were from old men's tales. Nothing like that could really happen to *him*.

"How's the Boss gonna know how long it took us to find them?" Pike objected. "We won't be long, and we won't cause him no delay. It ain't like he was waiting the whole herd on us. We'll just mosey up there and look around. Then we'll pop them strays out the bush and hurry 'em back. Ain't nobody gonna know we took a little time off."

"Yeah!" Snuffy agreed.

Vern shook his head. "Likely you won't find nothing."

"All right," Pike grunted in exasperation. "Then *you* go and hunt out the beefs while me and the kid take a pasear up there. We'll meet you back on the trail before you can get in sight of the drag."

With that, he stood up, pocketed the gold he held, and stepped onto his horse.

Vern watched uncertainly as Snuffy mounted up too. He shook his head again, but he said, "Bedamned if I'm gonna do the work for all three of us."

Grabbing the reins of his roan, he swung on board and followed.

The gully was far too steep for horses. Working along the slope, it turned out to be a fair ride up to the notch in the ledge above. From a distance, Old Grizzly had looked almost as smooth as a horsehide sofa, and from below the washout hadn't seemed high at all. Once they started climbing, though, the ground got rough and broken by outcrops of stone. And the washout didn't seem to be getting any closer.

Vern's doubts grew stronger and stronger. Their business was cattle, not gold. Especially not some dead man's gold. He was on the verge of speaking up again, arguing, to turn back, when at last they came onto the ledge. He held his peace then, as they threaded through the trees until they were at the broken ground of the water run. It turned out to be a larger, deeper notch than they'd expected.

Sitting their horses at the edge of it, they could see well out across the broad valley. To the north, the herd was stretched out, moving slowly into the distance.

"We ought to be getting back real quick," Vern said.

Snuffy gazed at the herd and muttered, "That's a darn lot of cows, ain't it?"

"If we find us that gold, we could buy a herd of our own," Pike said. "You got any idea how much profit a man makes on a drive like that?"

Snuffy shook his head.

Pike wasn't too sure himself. He answered with a snort, "Damnsite more'n a dollar a day. And he don't risk his hide and wear his butt to the bone doing it, neither."

"If you don't like droving, why'd you sign on?" Vern asked.

Pike snorted again and stepped down off the horse. He looped his reins on a low limb and footed over to the brink of the washout. He was a lean man, a lank

8

hard-boned scarecrow poised on the edge of the cliff. Running a hand thoughtfully over the dark scruff on his jaw, he peered down.

The ground was rough in the notch, and grown over in places with scrub. It sloped sharply, and as he lowered himself over the edge, he gripped at the brush to be sure he wouldn't slide right on down. Bits of rock kept wriggling from under his boots and bouncing along the slope.

Snuffy dropped rein and took out after him. The kid was young and, eager as hell. He didn't pay quite so much mind to where he stepped as Pike did. Suddenly one of the big chunks of rock rolled from under his feet and took him with it.

"Snuffy!" Vern shouted as the kid went tumbling down the slope, his arms flailing wildly. It was pure reflex, without the hesitation of thought, that had the throw rope in Vern's hands. Automatically, his fingers built the loop.

The hoolyann rolled down the rope and closed itself around Snuffy's high boot. Vern's horse threw back against the tug on the saddle horn as its rider swung a leg over the cantle. Grabbing the taut rope, Vern walked it to the edge of the washout.

He peered cautiously over and saw the kid hanging head down, his face in the dirt. Wriggling, Snuffy pressed his hands against the ground. He twisted his neck and squinted toward Vern.

"Lordy," Pike muttered as he scrambled back over the bronk. He wrapped his hands onto the rope along with Vern.

"Gonna climb back or you wanna be hauled in?" Vern hollered at the kid.

Snuffy shook his head. His face was turning a bright red. Digging his elbows into the ground, he began to squirm. But he didn't seem to be having any luck getting his head higher than his heels, so Vern and Pike leaned gently against the rope and started to pull.

They dragged him feet first over the edge of the washout. Vern loosed his rope from the kid's boot and coiled it. He hung it back on his saddle, then turned to the lad again.

Snuffy was just lying there on his belly, his shoulders heaving as he drew deep breaths. When Vern started toward him, he lifted up on his elbows and scowled.

"You damn near pulled my leg off!"

Vern stopped short. "Hell, next time I'll leave you go."

The kid rolled over and sat up. He looked hard and mean at Vern for a moment. Then he grinned sheepishly and said, "Reckon you hauled my bacon out the ashes."

"Reckon I did," Vern agreed.

"That was a hell of a pretty throw," Pike commented.

Snuffy rubbed at his face. There were some right smart scratches under the dirt he'd picked up. He sighed, then looked to Vern again, his face still redder than the freckles that splotched it. Almost inaudibly, he mumbled, "Thanks."

Vern nodded.

Pike asked, "See anything interesting on the way down?"

"Didn't notice nothin'."

Vern hunkered at the kid's side. This wasn't good, he thought. There was no luck in messing around with a dead man's gold. He built himself a smoke, then offered Snuff the sack.

With shaking fingers the kid took it and started a quirly for himself. Vern shared a match with him and once they'd both dragged of their smokes, he again suggested, "How 'bout we go find them cows now?"

"Like hell," Pike called in answer. He was standing on the brink again, staring down the way Snuff had fallen. After a moment, he walked back and took the rope off his saddle.

"What you up to?" Vern asked him.

"There's something down there. Snuffy shook loose a lot of rock. Some of it shines yellow in the sun." He snubbed the bitter end of his rope to the trunk of one of the quaking aspens. Hanging onto the other end, he began to climb down into the gully again.

Vern and Snuffy both got up to watch him. They could see the glints of color he was heading for. They saw him work his way carefully toward them, then pause and take a wrap of the rope around his middle. Bracing against it, he began to gather up the speckles of metal.

"It is the lode?" Snuffy hollered at him.

A couple of minutes seemed to pass before he lifted up his head and called back, "Don't look like it. Looks like when you come down, you turned open another one of them old money pokes."

He went back to scrabbling among the rocks, stuffing the bits he gathered into his chaps pockets. Vern and the kid waited, and finally he came back up the rope, his face flushed and his eyes glittering.

"Nother whole rotten poke full of the stuff," he said breathlessly. "That old feller must of had a mess of it with him. He sure struck the lode somewheres."

"Where?" Snuff asked eagerly.

"Who the hell knows?" Vern said. "He coulda been coming or going hundreds of miles when he got bushwhacked by the Injuns. I sure don't see no rock growing around here that looks like the stuff the gold's bedded in."

"All right, so maybe we don't find the lode," Pike grumbled. "But *I* ain't leaving here till I'm sure we got all the gold he was packing around with him."

Snuffy nodded in agreement.

Vern looked off at the dark mass of beefs moving up the basin. They didn't seem to have gotten far. There was only about twenty head strayed, he told himself. It shouldn't be hard to catch 'em up with all three men working at it. No point in his trying to do that work by his lonesome. And all that gold . . . he could see the bulge of Pike's pockets. A man could have himself a hell of a time in Cheyenne with his pockets stuffed that way.

He sighed and nodded reluctantly. Maybe they could afford to waste a little more time digging. He sure didn't mean to go do all the work and then stand by watching Pike and Snuff have all the fun in town.

12

Agreed, they loosened their cinchas, hobbled the horses, and knotted their throw ropes firmly to tree trunks. Each with a loop snugged around his waist in case he should slip, they set out down the dry water run to search and dig.

At first they found more of the nuggets that had spilled when Snuffy took his tumble. But then the ground stopped giving to them. When they finally crawled back onto the ledge, they were tired, dirty and not much richer than they had been when they rode up from below.

Hunkering together, they smoked and talked it over. Vern felt satisfied with what they had. He'd convinced himself that this much was real. But more still seemed like a wild impossibility. And he still felt uneasy about it being a dead man's gold. But Snuffy and Pike were anxious to keep hunting for more.

After a mess of palaver, though, they finally owned that neither one had any idea where else to look. And eventually they allowed that Vern might be right when he suggested that the old Spaniard had only been packing the two pokes they'd already found.

Emptying their pockets, they spread their kerchiefs and divvied up the ore evenly into three heaps. Each with his own share, they went to collect the horses and ride on in search of the strays.

The red roan had wandered despite its hobbles. Vern found it nosed into the brush. When he bent to pull off the hobbles, he found something curious. There were a mess of rusted airtights, like somebody had camped on this spot for a while. And it sure wasn't the Spaniard.

He was certain those old fellers didn't pack their grub in tin cans.

He gave the rust heap a prod and saw that cans weren't the only garbage in the pile. There were bits of rotted hide, too, like the old leather sacks the Spanish gold had been packed in.

He nudged at them with the toe of his boot, then hunkered and sorted them with a stick. There was no trace of that white stone with the gold flecked through it.

Well somebody had been there before them, he decided. Whoever left those airtights had already searched over the ground, cleaning out those little hordes of gold. The two pokes they'd found had been pure luck, overlooked by the previous hunter. That was that. He couldn't see any point in mentioning it to Pike and Snuffy, so he mounted up and rode on out to join them. There were stray cattle to be located.

They separated as they rode downslope, meaning to comb through the brush for those wandering beefs. Vern turned toward a creek that tumbled off into the bushy outcrops on the north, while Pike swung due south, and Snuff rode straight ahead to look for some sign of the critters having passed in that direction.

A good distance along the creek the brush thinned out and the trees began to grow more dense. Vern didn't like that much. He was happy enough in the brasada where a man couldn't see past his horse's ears and had to depend on his nose and ears to tell him what was around him. And he felt real fine in the open land where a man could stand up on his saddle and see

14

for a couple of counties in any direction. But these damned woods — he could see a ways and then not see. There were all kinds of shadows that wiggled and danced in among the tree trunks. And there were damn-fool trees that trembled without hardly a breath of wind blew through them. They made the patches of sunlight under them flicker and jump enough to shy a yoke ox.

The red roan snorted and whipped its ears alertly, as unhappy about this strange country as its rider was. All around, the woods were full of unfamiliar scents and sounds, and jammed from top to bottom with spooks.

The trees were low limbed. Vern hooked a leg and hung himself down the side of the saddle to peer under them. He sniffed the air, hoping to catch the odor of steers. There seemed to be something yonder, inside a clump of brush, all hunkered down like a proddyhorn trying to hide itself. He couldn't catch scent of it, but he reined the roan over, meaning to flush it out if it was one of the beefs.

The old man crouched in the deep shadow of a stone outcrop. What he had just discovered didn't exactly come as a surprise. He'd been expecting something like it for years. He knew just what he intended to do about it. After all, this wasn't the first time it had happened. And he had known it was sure to happen again.

He squinted, silently cursing the vague blurriness of the scene below. Maybe his eyes weren't as sharp as they had been a time bade, he thought, but he could still handle a sneak thief when he run onto one. He could learn one a proper lesson, too, before he was done.

The figure of the rider he'd been watching disappeared into the trees. That didn't worry the old man, though. He told himself that he could still outtrack any man, white or red, this side of the Big Muddy.

Grinning slightly with anticipation, he spat on his thumb and rubbed the forward sight of the rifle he carried. But he didn't intend to use the gun unless he had to. There were other ways . . .

Cautiously staying to cover, he started down the slope.

CHAPTER
TWO

It wasn't a steer there inside those bushes. It was a boulder. A big weathered gray one. Vern snorted with disgust at the sight of it. Where the hell had those beefs got themselves to? He started to push on, then stopped and gazed at the rock. It looked like the thing had been branded.

Curious, he stepped off the horse and poked at the marks on the stone. Up close they didn't look like much — just some gouges so old they'd gotten slimy moss growing in them. But when he backed off a few steps and squinched his eyes, he could see them take a shape like a brand. Cross Three Arrow. He'd never seen that burned into a bullhide.

He told himself maybe it was a good sign. A sort of omen. Maybe that arrow was showing him the way the steers had drifted. He couldn't see any reason not to poke on over and find out. It pointed sort of north and up a bit. Mounting, he headed in that direction.

When he broke from the woods into a broad, open park, he halted. It was a real pleasure to see a flat piece of land again. And the grassy sweep showed him marks of trampling, as if maybe the critters he was hunting had ambled a ways into it.

He grinned when he saw the cow droppings. That arrow in the rock had been showing him the way sure enough. From the look of them, those droppings were real recent. The beefs couldn't be far away.

He studied the trampled grass, considering. The golondrino had sure took his bunchquitters for a long walk. They'd done a fair lot of grazing too. Eight now they should be holed up deep in the underbrush, chawing their cuds and comtemplating whatever it is cows think about when they get that faraway look on their faces.

They were a pretty well roadbroke bunch, accustomed to having men on horses raising hell and pushing them around. He decided his best bet would be to call Pike and Snuffy on over. The three of them could work in, locate the bunch and move them out, no trouble at all.

Leaning his head back, he gave a holler that should have brought the others quick enough, if they were in earshot. Likely they were, he figured. After all, he could hoot across a fair piece of ground when he put himself to it. Touching spurs to the roan, he moved on into the woods the way the sign led. Snuffy and Pike could find the same tracks he had, as well as his own. They'd follow right along and catch up to him soon. Maybe by then he'd have the critters spotted.

He sniffed the air and watched the roan's ears as he rode. Red should catch scent of the beefs before he did. Then those ears would stop that searching and point, true as any hound. Red was a helluva fine cowhorse.

The ears stopped. Red hesitated, poised and tense. Vern could feel the pounding of the heart in the animal between his knees. He hooked a leg and hung himself down the horse's side to peer into the underbrush. He couldn't yet see the shapes, but he caught the scent of the cattle.

He touched rein to Red's neck, meaning to circle wide so as to drive them from behind. As he swung through the bushes, he glimpsed another branded rock. Pausing, he gazed at it. This mark was another cross and arrow, but with a figure five between them. He wondered what it might be pointing out to him now.

Could these things have been that old Spaniard's trail marks? There'd been a lode somewhere for that gold to have come from. Maybe it was miles and miles away. Then again, maybe it wasn't. That ore was sure pretty. Helluva lot prettier than the hind ends of a herd of beefs.

He sat a while, his eyes on the marks in the rock, as he thought. The kerchief-wrapped ore was a lump in his chaps pocket. He'd come to accept the reality of it. Now he remembered what Pike had said about how a man could buy himself one hell of a time in Cheyenne with a handful of that stuff. A whole lode of it? Hell, a man could buy himself a lot more than just a bust in town. A spread of his own, maybe. A waterhole and a house and a mess of stock beefs. He could hire some other damnfool to ride through the thorns after the proddies while he set up in the shade counting round dollars. He could ride up to the railhead in style while somebody else ate dust in the beef-critter's tracks, and then bust the town wide open like a ripe melon.

Glancing down at his toes, he thought as how a man might even buy himself a new pair of handmade boots with fancy carving all over them. And spurs with real silver jangle-bobs. If the lode looked anything like those samples the Spaniard had been carrying — even split three ways there would be more money than they could spend in a year or two of Sundays.

He reminded himself that he was a drover, in hire and on the Boss' time, hunting beefs, not gold. But he answered himself that the beefs were nigh found right now. About all that was left to do was round them up and get them back to the herd. They had their bellies full, and plenty of graze and water close by. They wouldn't be inclined to wander far. Gigging Red, he headed in the direction the arrow pointed.

There was no use sniffing the breeze now, or cocking his ear for the rustle of branches. He wasn't hunting animals this time. Now he had to keep his eyes open for another branded rock, or some sign of an old dig.

He had hooked his leg and hung himself down the side of the saddle again. He was riding slowly, studying the ground and bushes, not paying much attention to anything else. He didn't notice when Red cocked his ears back and listened as if there were something following behind. He didn't pay any mind at all to the faint sounds of movement in the brush. He just kept gazing into the shadows.

Until suddenly everything went black.

Even before he got his eyes open, Vern realized he couldn't move. Something seemed to have him down and was holding him spread-eagled on his back with his head lower than his heels. There was a sharp lump digging into his spine. Half-aware, he tried to shift himself off it, but he couldn't.

His eyelids were showing yellowish red. He forced them open a crack and saw the sun, full in his face and awfully close. It was damn near as hot as out on the desert. But the air still had that funny thin green smell of the mountains. He wasn't at all certain where he might be. Maybe asleep and dreaming, he thought.

The sunlight cut sharply into his eyes. He squinched them shut, then twisted his neck. At least he could move his head. Venturing to open his eyes again, he saw his own arm. It was stretched straight out from his shoulder and there looked to be a thong knotted on his wrist. It spanned a couple of feet from his arm to a stake stabbed into the rocky ground. And it was soaked wet.

He cursed aloud as he understood. He didn't have to look to know that his other wrist and both ankles were staked the same way. It was a damned Injun trick, spread-eagling a man with wet rawhide. As the sun's heat dried them, those thongs would shrink down, slowly pulling him apart at the joints. A goddamned Injun trick!

He tried to bend his elbow. The muscles bunched hard in his arm. There was a little give in the damp thong. Not much though. Not enough to do any good. The stake was driven in solid. And the loops around his wrist just dug into his flesh as he pulled.

He relaxed his arm and let his head down again, closing his eyes against the fire of the sun. It wasn't real, he thought. Nobody was doing this to *him*. Nobody had any reason to. But something inside him screamed back that it was real. This wasn't just some trooper's windy about the Injun Wars.

It was happening — to him.

Panicking, he strained at the thongs, twisting and heaving his body like, a pigged steer. Then, like an exhausted steer, he lay quiet, gulping the thin air into his lungs.

He swallowed at the hot panic and tried to think. Fighting those bonds wasn't doing him a damned bit of good. He couldn't bull himself loose. He had to use man-sense.

Turning his head, he looked at his pegged-down arm. He was able to bend it a bit. When he straightened it and pulled against the tie, he could lift the other shoulder clear of the ground. The thongs were still slack enough for him to squirm around. If only he could get his teeth into those knots . . . why the hell did a man have to have such a short neck anyway?

He jerked with his wrist again. Was the hide getting harder already? It wouldn't take long — not under that blazing sun. His desperate fingers dug into the ground under them, but found only gravel.

Craning his neck, he looked around. He seemed to be in a small bare spot, flanked on one side by a rise of rock. Above, he could see the bare granite face of old Grizzly real close. He was damned high up here. Tilting

22

his head back as far as he could, he saw nothing but sky.

He didn't see sign of man in any direction. It looked like whoever had staked him had gone off, not waiting around to watch the fun. He cursed again, then hollered. Maybe Pike or Snuffy would hear him.

His shouting sounded small, lost in the vast emptiness of the sky. His voice grated in his throat.

He rested his head, thinking maybe that bellering would only serve to bring back whatever damned Injun had staked him here. Well, if it did, that was that. He'd holler his head off. And if they shot him to shut him up, it would still be better than getting pulled apart slow by those drying thongs.

After a couple more shouts, he paused to listen. There was nothing to be heard except the wind. Sniffling, he scented only the odor of damp rock and woods.

With his chin dug into his chest, he looked toward his feet. The loops that held his ankles had been tied over his boots. There was still enough slack in the hide for him to bend his knees slightly.

He concentrated on his right foot, trying to dig the rowel of the big Mexican spur into the ground. There didn't seem to be anything under it but rock. And then he felt it bite, sinking in deep, catching as if it had found a crack in the stone. Braced against it, he began to work his foot.

The boot was tight. Why the hell had he bought such damned tight boots? At least they'd stretched a mite since they were new. But was it enough? He felt his heel slip a bit against the boot — then his foot bound tight in the instep. Cursing, he struggled at it.

He seemed to feel the hide shrinking tighter on his wrists. The air was cool, but dry, and the sun was close. It was hot enough to suck the dampness out of that wet hide like a thirsty steer. How much longer did he have before it began to pull his bones loose one from another?

He felt his heel slip a hairbreadth more. Tense, unbreathing, he worked at it. And then suddenly it was sliding straight out of the boot

He swallowed deep as he looked at his bent knee. That foot was free now. That leg was his again. But it was no good to him without the other one, and his hands as well. He slapped the bare heel down on the other boot to brace it and began to wiggle his left foot.

He had an infinitely long, horrible thought that that hide had tightened too much around that ankle. But finally the foot slid out and he could bend both knees. He sighed and tried to shake some of the sweat off his face. Now at last he didn't have to worry about getting his legs pulled off — only his arms.

Twisting his shoulders, he looked at his hand. The thong around his wrist was sure tighter. He couldn't twist himself over nearly as far as he had before. And the hide was cutting into his flesh now. He flexed his fingers. How the hell could he get his hands loose? He sure couldn't slide them out the way he had his feet. He'd have to find some way to cut those damp thongs.

He thought of the clasp knife that was as close as his pocket — and as far away as forever. It seemed almost

24

incomprehensible that something as simple as reaching into his pocket for it could be as impossible as it was. He mumbled soft curses as he gave up on thoughts of the knife and scanned the ground for something — anything — that might help.

There were bits of broken rock. One large shard caught his eye. It was too far from his fingers for him to grab hold of. Way too far, but . . .

Shoving his heels hard against the ground, he tried to bend his body to the side. One heel and then the other, he worked his feet, twisting himself. His spine felt like it was beginning to kink and his left shoulder to tear apart. He just didn't bend any further in this direction. But he had to.

One heel and then the other — and with his head craned around till his neck felt likely to snap, he saw his right foot close to the rock shard.

Digging his teeth into his lip, drawing a slow deep breath, and struggling to hold his patience, he inched his foot along the ground. His hip joint felt like it was going to wrench loose. He just didn't bend any further in that direction either.

A finger's width more would do it, he thought. Was that damned little distance going to break him? He dug his left heel hard into the ground. He had to brace strong against it to hold himself twisted the way he was. The thongs on his wrists were stretched taut, hauling back at him, trying to untwist him — or unloose his joints.

He managed to give the rock a kick.

It wasn't much of a shove, but the slope was down toward his head — and toward his hand. The bit of rock wobbled slowly downward. He cursed it and bullied it, as if it were a stubborn beef. It rolled. And stopped against the heel of his hand.

He let his body straighten out. With a protest of pain, his joints untwisted themselves. His lungs uncramped and dragged in air.

When he tried to move again the thongs were so tight that he could barely get his left shoulder off the ground. It took a lot of effort to raise his head enough to see the rock where it rested against his hand. The upturned edge showed jagged and sharp. Struggling, he got his thumb over it and eased it into the clutch of his fingers.

His hand was unresponsive. But at last he had the stone turned in his fingertips until the sharp edge lay against the span of hide. He could hardly move his wrist. The motion had to come from his fingers as he sawed it against the thong.

The knots were drawing tighter. The bonds pulled at his shoulders flattening them against the ground. The loops around his wrists were dug deep into his flesh and the feeling was leaving his fingers. He cursed again, lips moving in an inaudible string of accusations against the bit of rock and the hand that held it, against the thong and the man who had tied it.

Remembering good times and good fortune, he wondered if he could possibly have used up all his lifetime's worth of luck in such a few short years. There'd been trouble, close scrapes on the trail and in towns, but he'd always got out of them before. He'd vaguely assumed it would always be that way. He'd get out with a whole skin — wouldn't he?

Intent, he kept the stiffening fingers moving, rubbing the shard against the rawhide. Sweat trickled into his eyes, stinging and blurring his vision. His throat was so dry that when he gulped air, it went down in sharp-edged lumps. When he experimented again with hollering for Pike and Snuffy, his voice felt like a hoof rasp scraping inside his neck.

Sensation was completely gone from his hands now. He was numb clear to the elbows. The pain was in his shoulders. They felt as if they were opening up at the joints, bone barely held to bone by the lashings of pain. Only his legs were still alive and under his control. Twisting his hips, he pounded his heels against the earth. It hurt — but somehow it helped too.

His sight had got so blurry he couldn't make out his hand any more. And he couldn't feel it. He couldn't tell whether his fingers still moved at sawing the rock across the thong or not. But he concentrated on the thought.

The sun had been sneaking across the sky. Now it was hanging just above the granite face of Old Grizzly, a hot yellow blob that looked to sway from side to side like the tail of a clock, keeping time with the beat of his heart.

He could still feel the heart thumping in his chest all right. It was banging on his ribs and jerking at his shoulders. He halfway expected each jolt of it to tear his arms out at the roots.

As he closed his eyes against that vision of the swaying sun, he realized that he could no longer lift his head. His whole upper body was stretched taut between the shrunken thongs now. He couldn't move his shoulders at all. Trying only intensified the pain.

His legs were still free. He was aware of them writhing, the heels digging at the earth like the chopped-up pieces of a snake that wouldn't die until the sun set. They didn't seem to be connected with his mind, though. He wondered with a strange abstraction — if it would take him until sundown to die.

Something snapped.

He felt himself suddenly rolling, his left arm being twisted under him. For a moment he thought it was his right shoulder that had pulled apart. The pain in it was smothering every other feeling he had. It roared through his whole body like a flash flood down a gully, piling into red heaps inside his skull, trying to bust it open.

He fought it. With effort, he rolled himself onto his back again. His right arm was free, but it had no feeling. It hung from his shoulder like a dead log,

Finding some command over his heels, he dug them in and shoved himself toward the stake that held his left hand, easing the tension on the thong. For a long while he just lay there. At last the pain in his shoulders began to fade.

When he struggled to sit up, his head went to spinning. He sat with it hung down, his chin against his chest, until the spinning stopped. Slowly, his brains settled down inside his skull. He was able again to move his head without the feeling that they were slopping around, about to spill out.

28

He wiped his face against his shoulder. Blinking, he got his eyes to working after a fashion. Through a red haze, he could see his right hand hanging there on the end of his numb arm. Bending up his knees, he managed to get his arm across them. The thong was cutting deep into the flesh of his wrist. He dug his teeth into it found the knot and began to gnaw.

When it finally came loose, he jerked the strip of rawhide out of the gouge it had dug for itself and spat it away. Pain flooded into his hand, so intense that he doubled over, gripping the hand between his body and his thigh. His teeth were locked into his lower lip, filling his mouth with a taste of salt. He could feel tears squeezing from his clenched eyelids and trickling down his cheeks.

The hand came back to him. Slowly the pain eased and feeling took its place. The fingers responded to his desires. They were awkward, but they worked. He dug them into his pocket and found the clasp knife. Biting out the blade, he forced it under the hide that wrapped his left wrist.

There was the same pain, the same waiting doubled over fighting against it while his eyes seeped more tears. And at last that hand came back to him too.

He wiped at his face with a sleeve. The reddish haze faded from his eyes, though the things he looked at still seemed blurred. Resting his arms across his knees, he studied the damage.

The marks of the thongs were grooved deep into his flesh. His right wrist had chafed as he sawed with the stone. There was blood caked on it. The hands were stiff and swollen. But at least they were still attached to his body.

He leaned his forehead against one arm and let his eyes close. Suddenly he was weak all over — too weak to move. His bones hadn't got pulled apart at the joints, but they'd melted inside him. They'd turned to water and he could feel the chill of it trickling through his veins. Despite the heat of the sun on his skin, he shivered. He was cold, damned cold, down deep inside.

He forced his head up again, blinking and telling himself that this was a hell of a time to lose his nerve. He had to get moving before whatever damned redskin had staked him came back to see how many pieces he'd been pulled into.

There was an ache in his head that throbbed with the beating of his heart. It was like the clapper of a bell clanging inside his skull and ringing in his ears. Maybe if it hadn't been for that he'd have heard footsteps. But he didn't hear anything.

Leaning a hand on the ground, he started to get up. That was when he caught the scent. And suddenly something butted him between the shoulder blades. Something that felt godawful like it might be the muzzle of a gun.

It smelled like an Injun — the mixed scents of human sweat, rancid tallow and old leather. Holding his body stock still, Vern slowly turned his head. From the corner of his eye, he could see a fringed buckskin sleeve.

"You're a damned clever one, ain't you?" the old man said.

30

Vern moved slightly, just enough to get a look at the face. It was almost hidden by a scruffy white beard that showed deep streaks of sunburn. The skin was tanned dark, as scrubby and cracked as unkept leather. The eyes were a watery blue, reddish at the lids.

The old man wasn't an Injun. But he looked mean as one. There was a trade rifle in his right hand, the long arched hammer back under his thumb. He prodded the barrel at Vern's spine.

His voice raw in his throat, Vern asked, "You're the one who done this to me."

The old man nodded, grinning a bit.

"Goddamn hell of a way to kill a man!" Vern heard himself shout. "Why can't you put a bullet in him clean and decent?"

"Mebbe I will," the old man said. He sounded amused.

"It ain't human to stake a feller out that way!"

"Don't look like it worked none too good neither. How'd you get loose?"

"Chawed my way out! What the hell'd you do it to me for?"

"L'arn you a lesson. L'arn you not to go poking around where you ain't got no business."

"I got business here," Vern protested. "I'm looking for beefs that strayed off from our herd."

The old man snorted like he didn't believe it.

"'Bout twenty head of prime Texas proddyhorns," Vern told him. "You ain't seen them, have you? Being led by a big golondrino steer earmarked with an undercut right and half-cropped left. All of 'em road-branded CW on the left flank."

The old man worked his jaw and spat. Then he answered, "Nope."

Rubbing at his wrists, Vern glanced toward the lowering sun. "I better get the hell busy and find 'em. Got to get them back to the herd. If I can find my horse."

"Ain't seen your beefs, but I got your horse. Right nice-looking cayuse. Ain't had me no horsemeat in a long time."

Not Red, Vern thought. Red was too fine a cow-working horse to go for table meat. "If you've laid hands to . . ." He started to his feet as he spoke. But the gun muzzle pressed sharply into his back, stopping him. And suddenly he wasn't angry any more. He was just plain scared. If this old coot would stretch a man out to die slow and ugly, he sure wouldn't hold back from putting a rifle ball into him.

"Look here, Mister . . ." His voice came out all stringy and cracked. Where the devil were Pike and Snuffy? Hadn't they heard him hollering? He had a sick feeling that maybe they hadn't.

It seemed as if he could feel the old man's gnarled finger tightening on the trigger. He shouted, "What you want to go kill me for? You've learned me my lesson! I'll get off your mountain!"

"Nope. Too late now, boy. You'd tell 'em and they'd come swarming up here like the locusts. Can't have that happen. Not when I'm so close."

"Tell who what? I don't know nothing!"

32

"Like hell you don't." The old man fished his free hand inside the greasy buckskin jacket he wore. He brought it out with something clutched in the claw-like fingers. When he spread them open, Vern recognized his own bandanna the one he'd wrapped his share of the Spaniard's ore in.

"Gold?"

"Gold!" The white-whiskered grin broadened; "Gets in your bones, don't it? The sight of it sets you to boiling inside. You can't stop looking at it. Or for it. That's what you're really looking for on my mountain, ain't it? You think you can find that Spanish gold mine up here, don't you, boy?"

"Hell, no!" Vern said fervently. Right at that moment it was the simon-pure truth. "Mister, I'm a drover. All I want is to find my stray stock and get back to the herd."

Anger flashed across the ancient face, wiping away any trace of a grin. "Don't lie to me, boy!"

"I ain't lying!"

"Like hell you ain't. It makes you boil inside, the sight of that gold! Makes you so you can't hardly think of nothing else — only just finding the lode. I know just exactly how you feel, boy."

Vern shook his head in denial.

"Only *you* ain't gonna find it," the old man went on. "And you ain't gonna talk about it to nobody else neither. You ain't gonna send no sneak-thieving stake jumpers up poking around my digs!"

"Oh Lordy," Vern muttered. He clenched his fingers, then opened them to gaze at his knuckles. They were crisscrossed with the scars of grass ropes and the thorny brasada of south Texas. Dammit, he'd give all the gold in the whole mountain to be back in the middle of a chaparral thicket right now. Even with some damn proddyhorn trying to hook his horse out from under him. Why'd he ever left home to go droving anyway?

He could feel the cold touch of the rifle on his spine. The old man was holding it pressed hard into his back. Over his shoulder, he took another long look at the bearded face.

Real old, he thought, studying the seamed skin, the rheumy eyes and hunched shoulders. Standing hipshot, the old man gave the impression that one leg might be twisted a bit.

Maybe this hermit was a little bleary-sighted and a little stiff in the joints, Vern thought. Drawing up one leg, he braced himself. Maybe the old feller was making a mistake pushing that gun into his back, standing so close . . .

"You ain't yet found the lode yourself?" he said, trying to keep his voice steady. He wanted to distract the hermit, if he could.

The aged eyes narrowed down into a suspicious squint. "Just what do you know about . . . ?"

Vern jumped. Driving himself with one leg, twisting at the hips, he turned himself away from the gun — around it with his shoulder slamming the side of the barrel. He threw himself toward the old man's knees.

As he hit those legs, the rifle roared over his head. He thought he felt the bullet skim the folds of his shirt.

He'd moved quick and he'd hit hard. The old man's legs buckled. Vern felt him going over backwards. He sprawled with Vern on top of him, both hands grabbing for the neck behind that scrubby beard. But there was strength in the ancient bones — more than Vern expected. A sharp knee caught him where it hurt. He winced, grunting with pain.

The old man was trying to kick him again. Scrambling, he rolled full over onto his face. And then he was struggling up to his hands and knees.

From the corner of his eye, he glimpsed the old man rising, clutching the rifle by the barrel with both hands. That gun might be empty now, but it wasn't useless.

Vern flung himself forward as the gunbutt swung like a club toward his head. It fanned his hair, whistling wind in his ears. Getting a leg under him, he lunged. He meant to run like the devil, before the old man could swing again, or ram a ball down the rifle barrel.

He fell.

The slope dropped off suddenly, and almost before he could realize it, he was over the edge and tumbling. Face against the sharp incline, he was sliding with his fingers grabbing at outcropping rock. He caught handfuls of rubble. It came loose in his grip as he fell.

Something hit him hard. It slammed against his side, just under the short ribs. For an instant it halted his fall, holding him suspended. Then it bent, yielding his body and he was sliding again, head first now. He threw his arms out in front of his face. There was thick brush right in front of him.

As he clenched his eyes shut, he hit. He felt sharp branches tearing at him, scraping and stabbing. He felt the impact of his arms against solid ground, then his whole body. Then he lay still, flat on his stomach with something poking into his chest. He was aware of that much. He knew he wanted to move off whatever was stabbing into him. But when he thought of moving and tried to tell his body to do it nothing happened.

That was wrong, he thought. It was bad. There was some reason why he shouldn't just lie there. But he couldn't remember what it was. And hard as he might try, he couldn't move at all.

CHAPTER
THREE

The old man stood frowning at empty space where his enemy had been an instant ago. He lowered the rifle and sighed, trying to loosen the cramp that clutched at his chest.

That damned towheaded sneak thief had been quicker than a cat, he thought as he leaned on the long gun. Too quick, but not smart enough. Gone right off the cliff, hadn't he?

As the old man took a step pain surged through his bad leg, locking his knee. He cursed, lips moving silently. A man might talk to himself, but he was a fool if he did it loud enough for anybody else to hear. Using the rifle for a staff, he limped to the edge of the slope and peered over.

It was a long, steep fall. At the bottom, the carpet of brush was broken. He could see the hole in it and the blur of color that was the towhead's red shirt. With nothing to break it, a fall like that could kill a grizzly bear, he thought with satisfaction. That thief wouldn't be climbing up the mountain again. Served him right, too. Claimed he was a cowhand when any man, even one with a fuzziness to the eyes, could see he was nothing but a lowdown ornery claim jumper.

Leaning heavily on the gun, the old man squinted at the speck of red and told himself he should go on down and take a close look. Make sure the intruder was dead. But it was a hard climb down and his bad leg sure did ache.

He considered the possibility that the towhead might still be alive, but it didn't seem likely. He knew he should make sure. But aching the way he did, the old man wanted nothing more than to stretch out on his own pallet and rest. The cave where he made his home was upslope from here. To clamber down the cliff, then up again, would be a job of work, even for a young man with a sound body. For him now, it would be torture. But maybe he could be sure without going to the work of climbing down.

His gnarled hands measured powder from the horn he carried, judging it by feel as much as by eye. He loaded it and then the wadding and ball into the barrel of the rifle, then rammed them home. Just a drop of powder in the pan and the gun was ready. He lifted it to his shoulder. As he looked along the barrel, the patch of color in the brush grew fuzzier around the edges. He squinted to make it come clear and the front sight disappeared into a blur. He didn't have to see his sights to know where the familiar old gun was aimed, did he?

He took his time, fondling the weapon. Just so to the right — she threw leftward a bit — then, hammer back, his finger tightened on the trigger.

The stock bucked against his shoulder as the gun spewed hard sound and powdersmoke. It burned his eyes, drawing water and making the world look even more blurry. He cursed that, but the sharp singing scent of the smoke pleased him. Lot of fine memories in that smell.

Seemed like his memory was getting stronger these days, he thought. Oh, sometimes he forgot a thing that had happened last season, or even yesterday, but it was getting to where he could recall a lot more of what he'd done and where he'd been in the old days. He could remember how it was when his legs were strong and straight. He'd had good legs — walked a lot in those days. Covered a lot of land, hunting gold, sometimes finding it. Had him some roaring good times getting rid of what he'd found. Never had struck the mother lode, though.

But now he was close to it. He felt certain the Spanish mine was the lode he'd dreamed of all his life. Damn that towhead coming up here trying to take it away from him. He'd learned that one a lesson, though, hadn't he?

For a moment he couldn't remember just what he'd done to the intruder. He leaned on the rifle, frowning uncertainly. Then he recalled and took a look over the edge of the slope. The patch of bright red still lay motionless in the brush below.

Satisfied, he gave the rifle an affectionate pat. Then lamely, using the gun for support, he started back up toward his cave. He'd sleep well tonight, secure in his stronghold. He'd sure learned that one a lesson, hadn't he?

★ ★ ★

From somewhere beyond the misty darkness that enfolded him, Vern heard a shot. He had a vague feeling the bullet had been meant for him. But the echo died away and as best he could tell he hadn't been hit. He wasn't sure, though. He hurt so much now that he couldn't be certain he'd feel a bullet if it did hit him.

Something within him told him that, pain or no pain, he shouldn't just be lying there. He ought to get himself away. There was danger close by. There might be another shot — one that he would feel.

He struggled himself up onto his arms and forced open his eyes. They didn't seem to be working very well. Everything he saw was muzzy, as if he were under water. He got a hand up and wiped at them with his knuckles. It helped some. He could make out that he was in a thicket, a dense one that pressed in on him from every side.

It felt like something was stabbing him in the chest. With effort, he rolled himself off the broken stump of a bush. Above, he saw the blue of open sky. A vague piece of thought warned that was bad. He should get himself into cover.

Digging in his elbows, he dragged himself forward, away from the sky. He worked his way along on his belly, deep into the brush like a ladino trying to hide. Then he lay still, catching his breath and counting his arms and legs. They all seemed to be there.

He found he could move the legs but he couldn't get himself up onto them. He gave that up and pushed again, working his way further forward, crawling like a slinking varmint.

He kept his face close to the dirt, trying hard not to stir the brush overhead. Memories of the old man had come back to him and he wondered if the hermit might still be up on the ridge above, watching for sign of him. Had to stay to cover, he told himself. Had to find Pike and Snuffy. Funny how different the ground smelled here from that in Texas: Had a wet, musty scent to it. Funny how it kind of swayed.

And then it tilted over. It slopped right on upside-down. He was falling again, spinning headfirst. But this time it was a spiderweb soft blackness he plunged into. He didn't even try to stop himself.

Awareness came back slowly. Some damn feisty bronc had pitched him. That was his first thought, but even as it took shape, he decided that hadn't been the way of it. No, he recollected he'd fell off a mountain.

He lay still remembering the crazy old man who'd meant to kill him. Suddenly the face was vivid in his mind. And he recalled every tortured moment of getting himself out of the hermit's rawhide deathtrap. It had seemed like some kind of loco nightmare while it was happening, but the memory was starkly real. It shocked him awake.

He opened his eyes — but saw nothing. The darkness was stony pitch-black. But he *knew his* eyes were open. With a sense of panic twisting in his belly, he wondered whether the darkness was only night — or something else.

It *swelled* like night, he told himself. And it sounded like it. He didn't know names for all the critters that prowled the dark here in the high country, but that low

41

far-off song he heard, that was a coyote talking out its miseries.

Leaning on his arms, he tried crawling forward again. He ached. Moving made it worse. Every damn inch of him hurt. His bottom ribs on the left felt like a bronc had trod on them. His chest was sore as if he'd been stabbed. His shirt seemed to be shredded into tatters. And his eyes — he didn't want to think about them. That darkness might *not* be night.

He concentrated on taking inventory of the rest of his body. The chaps had given some protection to his legs. The joints were stiff, but not so painful as a lot of the other parts of him. He got one leg under him, then the other. Kneeling there in the brush, he listened. All his thrashing around had quieted the closest critters. He breathed deep of the air, but there was no human scent on it. The slim breeze brought a damp odor like rain clouds, and the green and small animal smells of the woods. Nothing more. That old man had been downright gamy. Vern felt confident he wasn't anywhere nearby, or upwind. He decided to chance standing up, if he could manage it.

Reluctantly, complaining with pain, his body answered his commands. He got his head and shoulders above the thick growth of brush. With a deep sigh of relief, he discovered that he could skylight the peak of old Grizzly. But the glow was faint. The sky seemed to be clouded over. He couldn't spot a speck of a star.

He *could* see, though. That was the important thing.

42

Struggling to his feet, he discovered that he could stand, but he couldn't walk worth hell. Each step shocked his banged-up side. He staggered a few strides, then gave up and sat down again.

It was awful quiet, and darker than a cow's insides at fly time. Listening, he picked out one single sound that held steady. It took him a moment to figure out that it was water running over rocks. That put him in mind that his throat felt as dry as ten miles of bare llano. He could have chawed prickly pears with the spines still on. Judging the direction by ear, he headed for the water on his hands and knees.

He found it and dipped his fingers into it. The handfuls he scooped up from the little stream tasted sweet. Stretching out on his belly, he put his face into it and drank deep. He let it wash over his skin. It felt good — cold and crisp, sucking away the pain.

Pleased, he tried exploring the stream with his hands. He could reach the far side if he stretched out his arm. When he touched his fingertips to the bottom, it only came up to his knuckles. It ran fast, though, and it eased the hot, stiff feeling in his swollen hands.

After he'd drunk again, he got to his knees and began working at the buckles on his chaps. When he finally coaxed them open, he stripped the chaps off and stretched out in the stream. Resting his head on his arm, his face was just clear of the water. It soaked into his Levi's and shirt, washing at the aches in his body, soaking them away.

Something tapped him on the back. He started like a spooked horse. Then something else was tapping at him and he realized it was rain. Big, dusty-wet drops of it were spattering on him. He glanced up at the darkness and they hit him in the face.

At first he didn't mind. He was sopping wet already. But the drops began to come thicker and faster, until they were pounding down. And the water in the crick was rising. Resenting the bother, he dragged himself onto the bank and crawled into the brush, dragging the chaps with him. Up close to the roots of a bush, he found earth that was damp but not muddy. The rain trickled from the leaves onto him, but they stopped it from battering at him. And the wide leather chaps were decent enough cover. Curling himself up in them, he drifted into sleep.

Pike and Snuffy had passed through the meadow where fresh cow droppings stained hoof-trampled grass. They had followed Vern's tracks, reading easily that he'd dismounted to examine a rock with a cross-five-arrow gouged into its face. They'd studied over the rock themselves, then ridden on, watching Vern's sign. Then suddenly something had muddled his tracks. His horse had stamped over a lot of grass. From there it had cut sharply away and its hoofprints had been lost in a small crick. As hard as they'd tried, they hadn't been able to locate the trail again. So they had returned to the marked rock, hunting in the direction the scratched arrow pointed.

It showed them the way to still another stone carved with similar markings, this time a cross-two-arrow. When they searched there for some sign of Vern, they found nothing.

Rising in his stirrups, Pike sniffed the air. "Gonna rain tonight." His voice mixed disgust and anger.

Snuffy took a deep breath. He couldn't be sure about the rain-scent, but Pike sounded positive. And the sky above Old Grizzly was turning a wild array of colors, now that the sun had disappeared past the peak. Clouds, thick and heavy, were moving in from the west. Pike was right about rain, he thought with admiration. He nodded agreement.

"Gonna wipe out any trail Vern might have left," Pike added.

"I'm real sure I heard him hollering a second time. Snuffy said. Vern's first call had been clear enough. They'd both heard it, and had followed it to find the cow droppings. The second time a couple of hours later, Snuff had only heard a faint noise from a far distance. Pike denied it was a man's voice. Some kind of bird, he'd insisted.

Now Pike said firmly, "He didn't holler for us no second time."

"How you so sure?" Snuffy asked.

"Why would he have hid his sign the way he done if he *wanted* us to follow him? I tell you, he's been onto these here markers." Pike shrugged toward the rock that wore the cross-two-arrow brand. "He seen they were the old Spaniard's trail and he followed them. Now he's found the lode and he don't want us finding it, nor him either. He's struck it rich and he figures to keep it all for himself."

Snuffy frowned at the idea. "Why would he want to do that? We're all friends, ain't we?"

Eyeing the boy, Pike wondered how anyone could be so dumb. As if it were a complete and thorough answer, he said, "Gold."

It didn't make sense to Snuffy. Friends shared, didn't they? Hadn't he and Pike and Vern already shared what gold they'd found? If they could share that little bit among themselves, why couldn't they share a bigger find even easier? It sure wouldn't be fair of Vern to keep it all for himself. Not when they'd all ridden together and when it had been him, Snuffy, who'd found the old dead Spaniard in the first place. He shook his head in disbelief.

"Look," Pike said impatiently, "if Vern ain't trying to hide from us, why ain't we found his sign?"

Snuffy just looked at him blankly.

"He's found the gold and he wants to keep it to himself," he added.

Pike sure sounded like he knew what he was talking about, Snuffy decided. He said, "It ain't fair. We got a right to share in it."

Pike nodded, glad that the kid was showing some trace of sense at last. "Then I say were gonna find him and get it. No matter what!"

"All right," Snuffy mumbled.

Looking at the dying twilight, Pike sighed. "Well, we ain't gonna find him tonight. That's for sure. Reckon we might as well make camp here."

46

"I ain't got my bedroll," Snuffy protested. "Nor food neither. I'm *hungry*."

Pike gave another disgusted grunt. "Hell, we got our saddle blankets and slickers to roll up in. And we can go back and butcher us one of these steers for meat."

"One of *our* steers?"

"Why the hell not? They ain't important now, boy. We're on the track of gold. You understand that? *Gold!*"

Snuffy nodded. Likely Pike knew best. Leastways, he sounded real sure of himself.

"We'll fetch up on Vern tomorrow, all right," Pike was saying as he turned his horse. "We'll get our share of the gold. And I'll learn him to try stealing from his friends."

As Snuffy wheeled to follow, he wondered if it couldn't all be a mistake. He *thought* he'd heard Vern holler the second time. It was hard to imagine Vern trying to steal from them, the way Pike said.

Well, they'd find out for sure tomorrow when they caught up with him, the boy decided. For now, his main concern was the knot of hunger that had been growing in his belly. Seemed wrong to kill one of the Boss' steers, but Pike said it was all right. Pike ought to know, shouldn't he?

The old man woke with a start. He realized that he'd dozed off with his cup of tea only half-drunk. The lone pipe of tobacco he rationed himself each day had gone cold in his hand.

It had been a hard day, he told himself in excuse for falling asleep that way. Damned sneak thief prowling around *his* mountain, hunting for *his* gold. Wouldn't no stranger get that treasure, though.

No, he'd done for the towheaded intruder, staking him on the hill, the same way he'd done for the one who'd come nosing around last year. Or had that been two years ago? Must have been more'n that. Had been before he'd busted his leg. When was that? Four, five winters ago? He'd lost count. Didn't much matter, though, he told himself. Important thing was he'd got rid of the intruder.

He looked across the cave at the shadowy shapes of leather sacks heaped against the far wall. Been a long time since he'd first found the bones of the dead Spaniard up on that ledge, with those sacks of ore around him. Four pokes full. He'd camped there on the ledge, cleaning out the gold, hunting more. Then the land had broke away. The bones had gone tumbling down the slope. *That* was the same year he'd busted his leg, he thought, feeling a deep satisfaction at having remembered.

Taking a stick from his small fire, he relit the pipe and thought again of the towheaded intruder. He'd been lucky to spot the feller dismounting to study one of the marked rocks. And foxy to follow when the towhead rode off to find another one. Real clever to come up close and lay him across the skull with a hefty chunk of stone when he tried to look for the third one.

His chuckle turned to a sudden frown. He recalled now that he hadn't succeeded in killing that one by staking him. No, there'd been a tussle and the towhead had got away. Fell off a cliff, though. Seemed he recollected putting a bullet into the boy after that. Well, come morning, he'd go back down and take a look at the body. But for now he was satisfied that the gun had finished the job if the fall hadn't. His eyes might not be so good as they were once, but he could still shoot straight. Smiling to himself, he remembered a turkey shoot once, back when he was a young'un.

He gave a shake of his head as he realized he'd dozed off again. Been a hard day, he repeated, listening to the rain outside. Plenty warm and snug here inside his cave. There were drafts enough coming through the cracks and crevices in back to clear away most of the smoke, but they weren't bad enough to chill his bones. Damn fine cave. Well hidden, way up here on Old Grizzly.

Stiffly, he got to his feet. He stretched, then hunkered to bank the fire, saving the coals for morning. Then he lay down on his pallet, wrapping his weary aching body in an old buffalo robe. All he needed was a good night's sleep, he told himself. Had a chore to do come morning. Couldn't quite recall what it was. Oh yes, he had to make sure that the towhead was thoroughly dead.

The long rifle lay at his side. He patted it affectionately as he closed his eyes.

CHAPTER
FOUR

Vern woke feeling like he'd been six months riding night-herd on a bad run in a flood-storm. He was snuffly, aching, stiff and miserable. For a long while he just lay curled under the protection of the chaps, remembering how he'd come to be there.

His body was sore and his side painful where he'd struck an outgrowth of brush as he fell down the cliff face. But the fall might have been worse, his pains a damnsite worse, if that thing hadn't broken his fall.

He tried to scent the air, but snuffling the way he was, he couldn't pick out odors, so he lay still, listening. As best he could make out, the woods sounded natural, all full of little scampering and chittering noises.

Beyond the brush that covered him, he could see a small grassy park with a little crick bounding through it. A mule doe stood with her forefeet in the water. As he spotted her, she jerked up her head, glancing in his direction and disappeared. Purely disappeared.

It seemed like fair good odds that the crazy old hermit wasn't anywhere around, he decided. Gamy as that old man was, the doe wouldn't have got within half a mile of him in any direction. Satisfied that it was safe, he crawled on out of the brush and sat up. Stretching, he worked the stiff muscles of his shoulder and flexed his arms and hands. The swelling in his fingers was almost gone, and they seemed to work all right.

He got himself a mouthful of crick water, then looked up at the sky. Sure slept late. By now the herd would be strung out and moving along. Ashes in the breakfast cook pit would be cold. Hell, but it had been a long time since he'd ate last. Leaning his arms on his knees, he rested his head against them. He had some serious thinking to do.

To begin with, he was afoot and on unfamiliar ground. And he was unarmed. That old coot had took his hand gun and he'd dropped his claspknife up on the ledge when he'd felt the rifle nudge him in the spine. His boots were still on that ledge, too. The chaps had kept his Levi's in pretty good shape, but his shirt wasn't fit for saddle-oiling rags. All in all, he was nigh stripped down to nothing but the man animal. And a hell of a long ways from home.

Straightening up, he tapped a hand to his shirt pocket, not expecting to find anything. He didn't. The pocket was torn open, the tobacco sack and matches gone. But he'd reminded himself the hard way of that hurt spot on his chest. He widened out one of the rips in his shirt and took a look at it.

The broken bush stob had poked him hard enough to gash a hole in his skin, but it wasn't very deep. He'd got thorn-scratched in the maguey and agrite worse than that plenty enough times.

He explored a little further. His left side had an ugly bruise big as his hand and purple as a ripe prickly pear plum on it, but his ribs felt whole. Sore and aching as he was, he didn't seem to be busted anywhere.

What the hell, he told himself. After all, he'd been pitched higher and fell harder off them sandy-gullet Texas broncs plenty of times. Scooping his hands full of water, he drank again. Then he stood up and tried his Levi's pockets.

Something was still in there. He brought it out, looked at it, and grunted. The Jackson Cent he'd had since he was a kid. Hard times money, the way he'd heard. He'd carried it for a lucky piece, but damn lot of luck it had brought him this last couple of days.

He started to toss it away, then caught it and stuffed it back into his pocket. He was still alive, wasn't he? That old man had tried twice to kill him and he was still alive — not even busted up. How much luck could he expect from one old bad penny?

Slinging the chaps over his shoulder, he set out walking. Long as he headed downslope, he'd be going in the right direction, more or less. He was sure to either find Snuff and Pike, or else pick up the trail of the herd. He wondered if those two had rounded up the strays yet. Likely they had. Why the hell hadn't they found *him* yet? They ought to be hunting around now, looking for him. They sure wouldn't go back to the herd without him, would they?

Lordy, but he was hungry.

He came out of the woods into a broad, grassy meadow. It looked like the same one he'd found cow-sign in, but he knew it wasn't. The sun shone bright in his face, feeling real good. Warm and friendly,

52

not at all hot and murderous the way it had yesterday when it was shrinking up those thongs around his wrists. As he crossed the meadow, he could feel it heating away the sniffles. That was good. He began to catch the scents in the air again. Nothing that smelled of cattle or horses or men, though.

Walking in the open meadow grass was pleasant. But walking in the woods wasn't. As he entered forest again, he found the ground mostly covered with decaying leaves and beds of deep fir needles, but there were sharp rocks, broken branches and spiny pine cones mixed in. They tore at his bare feet. A sharp stone dug a gash that oozed blood.

He found another little click and settled to soak his feet in it. As he watched the water ripple over his toes, he told himself times were getting hard. At this rate, he couldn't cover much ground at a stretch. And he was helpless enough now, without his feet were to quit on him.

In the sky-clear water a long speckled fish paused to investigate his foot. He stared at it, wondering if he could paw it out like a raccoon would. He made a lunge to try, but it slithered away. Glancing around, he wondered which of the things that grew in the mountains a man could eat without they poisoned his gut. Hell of a thing to be lost in such strange country. He looked at his chaps, thinking as how chawing rawhide would ease a man's thirst. Would chawing a chunk of chap-leather do anything for his hunger?

Another thought came to him. He pulled a concho off the chaps and studied it over. A thin dished disk of steel close to two inches across. He rubbed it over a piece of rock, thumbed the edge and rubbed again. Damned if it didn't look like he could hone an edge onto it.

Letting his feet soak, he worked at improvising a blade. When the edge of the concho felt sharp enough, he tried making a cut into the leather of the chaps. The slice wasn't any too neat, but at least the concho did cut. Spreading the batwings, he began to hack at them. First a couple of good-sized pieces from their wide bottoms. Then he began carefully to cut the long spirals that would give him thongs.

When he'd finished, with the thongs laced through slits in the edges of the big pieces, he tied them onto his feet. And grinned at the results. A redskin would likely have laughed himself sick at the sight of those moccasins. But they looked like they'd work. At least, they should keep his feet from getting cut up any worse.

Feeling right pleased with his own ingenuity, he slung the remains of the chaps over his shoulder, pocketed the sharpened concho, and set out walking again. His feet still hurt enough to make him limp a mite, but it was sure better going than it had been on bare skin.

The woods stopped suddenly. So did the ground. He found himself on the edge of a couple of feet of sparse grass between the trees and a sharp drop-off. Standing there, he looked out over a wide mess of land.

From the ledge where he stood, the land dropped sharply, then rolled into a broad forest-covered slope. Beyond, way down, lay the valley, and across it another batch of peaks rose jaggedly into the sky. Up valley a ways, he could make out a dark smear that he figured must be the herd. It was moving away from him. He wasn't sure about judging distance in this high country, but he had a notion they were a lot further off than they looked. Maybe they'd run again last night in that storm. He'd bet the Boss was plenty burned about three of the hands not getting back with the strays by bedding time.

What land of story was he going to give the crew when he got back to the herd? It'd have to be a good one to explain how he'd come to lose everything but his britches. Might not be smart to let on about that Spanish gold, though. Some of the fellers would get gold fever for sure if they heard about it. They'd break loose to go hunt it and if he lost men to gold fever, the Boss'd get feisty as hell. Vern sure didn't want to be responsible for anything like that.

Hell of a thought — there was the herd still in sight and there he was looking at where he wanted to be, but there wasn't anything he could do about it except plod along like an old yoke ox, hoping eventually he'd catch up.

He was scanning the cliff face, wondering if there was any better way down than walking all the way to where the incline eased into a gentle slope. That was a right long way off, and he sure didn't feel like doing any more footing than he had to. Right steep cliff, though. Did something just move down there?

He squinted into the shadow of an outcrop on the rough face of rock. Yeah, he breathed softly in answer to his own question. It looked like old grandaddy rattlesnake curled up in the shade for a siesta. A big fat old granddaddy with a mess of knots on its tail and hefty meat on its ribs. He knelt to peer at the snake and study the situation.

It was eight feet down. Too far to reach, and bedamned if he wanted to go barehanding a rattler like that anyway. But with a rope, now . . . he didn't have a rope, but he had the next best thing. Pulling the knife-edged concho out of his pocket, he spread the chaps to cut himself another thong. This time a good long one. Better'n eight foot long.

The snake's head was flat against the rock. Vern couldn't figure any way to get at it. But the critter's tail was up, crossing over a coil of the body and sticking straight out in the air. It just begged to be lassoed.

He hunted himself up a forked stick. Then, with a slip knot in the end of the thong, he stretched out on his belly, his head over the ledge. Slow and careful, he lowered the loop. Real easy now — didn't want to wake up old man rattler — not till that loop was on him and snug.

It wasn't hard. The thong had enough stiffness to keep the loop open. He gave it a slight twist, then a sharp jerk, and the loop snapped tight around the knotty tail.

Granddaddy snake woke up sudden and angry. He slid right off the rocks, writhing like crazy at the end of the line. About six foot of pure hateful poison dangling there in space, Vern figured as he groped for the forked stick. A real handsome chunk of snake meat.

He kept the rattler hanging, playing it on the end of the thong, careful to keep it from getting itself gripped onto anything like a root stub or rock outcrop. With the line switched to his left hand and the stick in his right, he scrambled to his feet.

He jerked his catch in suddenly, swinging it at the end of the thong. As it smashed against the ground, he jumped. The fork of the stick slammed down astride its violently writhing head. He had it pinned.

It was a wild, squirming critter, lashing its whole body-length like a bullwhip as he bent to crush its skull with a rock. Even after he'd made pulp of the head, the body still twisted spasmodically. He glanced at the sky, thinking it was a long time till sundown when the rest of the snake would finally stop wriggling forever. Dammit, he didn't feel like waiting until the sun had set and the critter had finished with its dying.

He caught at the twitching body with his left hand. The muscle under the slick skin was rock hard. Rattler might be an ornery animal but a man couldn't help kind of admiring it. Sure had a fine hide, he thought as he gashed at its belly with the sharpened concho.

By the time he had a good piece of it skinned, the snake no longer twitched. Its meat seemed thoroughly dead. He was real glad for that. The idea of the thing squirming inside him till sundown sure hadn't done much for his appetite.

Even raw, it was good eating. And once he'd filled that nagging hole in his belly, Vern didn't feel near so bad about being afoot and lost on the mountainside.

He told himself he wasn't *exactly* lost. He knew where the herd was. He just had a long ways to go to get to it.

Settling on the lip of the cliff, he gazed at it in the distance. The warmth of the sun felt good on his back and there was sure a satisfaction in having a full belly again. After a few moments, he stripped off the tatters of his shirt and stretched out. Let old man sun bake some of his aches for a while. It sure felt good to rest.

He opened his eyes with a start. Must have dozed off. And to judge from the position of the sun now, he'd done it a couple of hours ago. Stretching, he yawned, then looked at the herd up valley. Sure didn't look like they'd moved to speak of. Hard to tell anything at this distance, though.

But *something* was moving. He caught a glimpse of it in the woods downslope. Squinting, he scanned the trees. There it was again. He let out a holler. It was one of the boys, either Pike or Snuffy.

He saw the rider's broad brimmed hat tilt, and knew his holler had been heard. On his feet now, he windmilled his arms and shouted again.

Calling back, the rider reined toward him and nudged the horse into a lope. Vern recognized him now. It was Snuffy, on the bay. Eager, he peered down the face of the rock looking for some way to get down to the kid. A man might climb that rough stone. Leastways, he could sure try.

Cautiously, he lowered himself over the edge. At first, he found foot and handholds easy enough. But then suddenly he seemed to run out of them. He'd gotten himself about halfway down and there he was — bellied up the cliff wall, hanging on with his fingertips and one foot; while the other groped, not finding a damn thing to set itself on. He squinted up at the rim overhead. A long ways up. He sure didn't feel like climbing back again.

Finally he worked up enough nerve to look down. Long ways that way too. Dammit, the things a man could get himself into! How'd he get hung up on a wall of rock this way anyway?

He glimpsed Snuffy pushing the horse through the brush and decided that he was going to get the rest of the way down somehow. Bracing the one foot that had a rest, he cautiously moved a hand to a lower hold. Then the other hand. Clinging, with the breath caught in his lungs, he stepped off the lone foothold.

For a long moment he hung there by his fingers, his feet feeling for something — anything — he could set them on. But they couldn't find a thing. And suddenly his fingers let go. He hadn't planned it that way. They just plain got tired and quit on him. With a screech of surprise, he slid down the face of the cliff.

He hit bottom in a shower of loose rock and dirt. His knees bent and he folded up, lying crumpled with the thoughts all blurred and busted up inside his head. Lordy, he felt like he'd been dragged by the stirrup and peeled his chest right off.

"Vern?" Snuffy's voice was soft and uncertain, as if he was afraid of waking the dead.

Vern grunted.

Snuffy stepped off the horse and bent over him. "Vern? You alive?"

"Hell, I don't know," he mumbled. Drawing breath he decided he must be. Nothing dead could hurt as much as he did.

Hunkering beside him, Snuffy asked, "What was you doing up there?"

He sighed, sort of groaning, and got himself busy with trying to sit up. Once he'd made it onto his rump with his back leaning against the rock, he squinted at the kid and asked, "You got the makings?"

Snuff looked completely bewildered as he fished out his tobacco sack and held it toward him.

"You roll it," he said. "I'm plumb wore out."

The kid built the quirly and got it lit for him. When he dragged on it, the smoke hit his lungs like a cow's kick. It set his head to spinning. But after a moment things straightened themselves out again.

"Where you been, Vern?" Snuffy said plaintively. "We been looking to hell and gone for you."

"Where's Pike?" Vern grunted.

"Oughta be on his way here. He shoulda heard me holler. Maybe seen you up there, too. What was you doing up there, Vern?"

"Hunting horse biscuits," he muttered. He didn't feel like talking about it. The whole business was kind of embarrassing.

"Where's Red?" Snuffy asked.

"Lordy, don't you know nothing but questions?"

The kid sat back on his haunches, looking a little hurt by the sharp tone.

"Hell . . ." Vern mumbled under his breath.

Something rattled the brash. Vern cocked an ear. It was coming toward them like a charging bull. He spotted the sombrero, then the rider. It was Pike, pushing his horse hard.

Jerking rein, he swung himself out of the saddle and bent to peer critically at Vern. "Where the hell you been?"

"Takin' a real close look at the scenery."

Pike eyed the raw gashes the slide down the slope had scraped into Vern's chest. "Scenery kinda took a close look right back at you, didn't it?"

"What'd you do with your boots, Vern?" Snuffy asked.

Vern ignored the question.

Pike squatted to look into his face. With a stone-edged seriousness, he repeated, "Where you been?"

"Up the hill a ways," Vern grunted. He didn't meet Pike's intent gaze, but stared at his own feet and the crude moccasins. He could feel the warmth rising in his face. He was damn near fresh-foaled naked, and these fellers wanted to know how come. It'd sure give them a laugh to find out some crazy old hermit had took his horse and gun and had cost him his clothes, wouldn't it?

"Where you been!" Pike demanded.

"It ain't none of your damn business," Vern snapped back.

Pike glanced toward Snuffy with a significant nod, as if this confirmed his worst suspicions.

The kid looked on blankly, thinking it might be that Pike was right about Vern and the gold. He wondered what Vern had done with his boots. It didn't make sense for a man to be walking around afoot like that without his boots.

"You found the lode, didn't you?" Pike said coldly.

Startled, Vern frowned at him. "Huh?"

"Don't try lying to me. You found that gold and you thought you'd keep it all to yourself, didn't you?"

"Like hell!"

Pike's top lip was drawn up into something like the beginning of a wolf-snarl. His dark eyes had a shiny look to them, as if he had a touch of fever. Puzzled, Vern glanced from him toward Snuffy.

The boy hunkered there, fingering, at the ends of the reins he held, watching with uncertain eyes.

"He took sick of something?" Vern asked, half-serious.

Instead of answering, Snuffy said, *"Did* you find the gold, Vern?"

"Like hell!" Something about the two of them — about the set of their faces, Pike's in particular — gave Vern a right uncomfortable feeling. He dragged at the quirly, feeling the strong smoke spread itself through him. "You really think I found the Spanish mine?"

Snuffy nodded slightly. And Pike demanded, "You trying to tell us you didn't?"

"Damn right I didn't!"

Pike's hand curled into a hard, threatening knot in front of Vern's face. "You gonna tell me the truth?"

"Sure," Vern muttered, staring at the hand. He didn't feel much like arguing. Especially not with fists. Not the way he ached. So what if they laughed, he told himself.

62

"Truth is, there's a crazy old man living up on this mountain. He got hold of Red and my gun and he tried to kill me. He's looking for that gold himself. He figured I was after it and he meant to kill me lest I found it. If you go nosing around for it, he'll likely try to kill you too."

Snuffy's expression turned to awe. But Pike's was marked with disbelief. He snapped, "You're trying to scare us off, huh? You think you can keep us from getting our share of that gold."

"You can have the whole damn lode, far as I'm concerned," Vern grunted. "All I want is to get back to the herd."

"You're gonna take us to the gold!"

"I don't know where it is."

Pike exchanged looks with Snuffy again. "I'm gonna have *my* share!"

Vern shrugged. "All right with me. But all your talking ain't gonna make it no different. I *don't know* where the gold is."

The disbelief was still in Pike's face. But he said, "We'll find it for ourselves then. And you're coming with us."

Vern started to protest. But he looked at his bootless feet and thought how far off the herd had looked from up on that ledge. Hell of a long way for a man to get without a horse. How long would it take Pike and Snuffy to get over this gold-hunting sickness and settle to going back where they belonged? Maybe not long. Likely a feller'd be better off sticking with them than wandering around nigh naked, trying to follow a trail herd afoot.

Sighing, he said, "I'll go with you. But I swear I ain't found that gold."

Pike gave a snort through his nose. As he stood up to reach for the reins of his horse, he grumbled, "We can go back to that last marker-rock and start over from there."

Looking happy again, Snuffy held a helping hand toward Vern. "You can ride up behind me. I'm pretty light and he's a good strong horse."

Vern nodded and accepted the help. His body didn't much want to move. He'd sooner have set and rested a while longer. But these two seemed downright determined and he sure didn't feel like arguing them.

Snuffy climbed into the saddle and Vern swung up to settle his aching bones behind the cantle. It was a good feeling to be astride again, even riding double.

CHAPTER
FIVE

The old man took his time making the trip down from his cave. He eased carefully over the rocks and across the slopes to the ledge where he had staked that towhead. There, he rested and thought about his tussle with the intruder. If it hadn't been for his bad leg, he told himself, he'd have showed that young 'un a thing or two about wrassling. He chuckled softly, remembering fights long past. Then he hobbled over to the edge of the cliff.

The brush below was a green carpet, battered by the night's storm. He peered at it, searching for a spot of red. Funny, but he couldn't locate it today. That puzzled him. He was certain the towhead's dead body was down there somewhere.

With a sigh, he started along the cliff's lip, looking for an easy place to climb. But the best course down that he could find was still steep and rugged. He had to stop to rest his leg several times. And at the bottom he had to break his way through the brush to get to the place where he'd seen the red shirt the day before.

It wasn't too hard to find the spot where the towhead had been lying. The undergrowth was broken as if it had been trampled. But the intruder was gone.

The old man shook his head in amazement. Was it possible the towhead was still alive? He searched, prodding into the brush with his rifle barrel. But all that he could find was a single shred of red cloth. Leaning on the gun, he tried to recall. He was positive he'd took a shot at that intruder. Could he have *missed?*

He ran a thumb over the gun's front sight, feeling a deep disappointment. After all the years he'd carried this rifle, living with it and loving it like kinfolk, could it have betrayed him? Squinting at the vaguely blurry images of the trees around him, he considered one other possibility. Maybe that towhead had somehow managed to hex the gun.

It was an answer that satisfied him. He hadn't been betrayed by the gun. It had all been the intruder's doing. Damn towhead must be a man-witch. The old man could remember how his ma had spoke of such kind back in the old country where she'd come from. They were sly and clever. But there wasn't any man-witch gonna outfox him! No sir!

Tucking the rifle under his arm, he patted it to reassure it and began casting about for some mark of the intruder and the way he'd gone. Finally he found a trail of broken brush near the crick, and a place under a bush that looked as if some animal had nested through the night. Not a woods animal, though, he thought with a slight grin. Nope, he was on the towhead's trail. And it wasn't gonna be hard to follow.

The sun was in the west by the time the old man reached a ledge overlooking the valley, and found bony remains of a rattler there. As he hunkered to study them, he heard sounds. They seemed to be coming up, rising on the breeze that rose over the lip of the cliff. And they were sounds that did *not* belong on his mountain.

Moving cautiously, he looked over the ledge. And recoiled in shock.

For a moment, he paused, wondering if his eyes had told him true. Then he looked again. There wasn't just one sneak thief come onto his mountain. There was *three* of 'em!

His lips twisted into a silent snarl as he watched. There were only two horses. The third man swung up behind one of the others. Blurred as the figures were, he couldn't be sure, but be thought that third one was the same towhead, shirtless now.

Gnarled hands raised the rifle to his shoulder. He gazed along its barrel, trying to see the mounted figures and some hint of the gun's front sight at the same time. But when he set his eye for one, the other would disappear completely. It was the hex working, he told himself.

The horses turned. The intruders were riding off, into the forest. *His* forest, on *his* mountain. He knew with his very bones that they were hunting his gold.

Lowering the gun, he leaned on it and considered. It wouldn't be no use trying to pick them off from here. They were already moving into the trees. Even if he did manage to hit one with the hexed gun, it'd give warning to the others. Long as they had that charm working, for them, he'd have to be real careful. Be best to track them. They'd have to make a camp for the night. He could sneak up on them then and pick them off one at a time in a nice quiet Injun style.

Grinning to himself, pleased with his own craftiness, he tucked the rifle under his arm and began to walk.

Misty twilight lay over the mountain by the time Pike finally reined in and said something about camping.

Vern blinked a couple of times and flexed his stiff shoulders. It was nigh time they stopped to rest. Up yonder, afoot and lost, he'd had an excitement in his blood that helped numb his aches and keep his head working. But found and on a horse again, he'd run out of energy. All he felt now was a sore weariness, harnessed to a strong urge for food and sleep.

Easing a leg over the horse's rump, he slid down from behind Snuffy and looked around. The woodsy brush they'd been traveling through ended here. He stood at the edge of a swath of rubble that flowed down the mountain's slope like a river of broken rock, frozen into place.

Glancing up, he muttered, "Sure looks like one helluva piece of that mountain broke off and come sliding down here." He hoped it wasn't likely to happen again soon.

Snuffy dropped out of the saddle and stepped to his side. "That's what Pike and me figured. That there slide ruint the trail for us."

"How come?"

"When we couldn't find your sign, we follered them arrows in the rocks. Got to here and knowed we should find the next arrow somewheres around close. But there ain't none. We gone over the ground good looking for it. Way we figured, the landslide must have took it off."

"Yeah," Pike grunted. He'd swung off his own horse and come over to them. His voice was a heavy, meaningful grumble. "Maybe come morning Vern can help us find it."

"I told you I don't know where that Spanish gold is," Vern said wearily.

Pike snorted again.

Vern just shrugged. If he hadn't felt so tired, he might have argued it a while. This whole business of the gold was a lot of damn foolishness to his mind. It was a dead man's gold and lost to the devil. A man with half the sense of a good roping horse would have known he was just wasting time hunting for it.

Turning to Snuffy, Pike said, "You get a fire going, eh?"

That reminded Vern of the hole in his stomach. He yawned deep and felt just how empty he was. He asked, "You got vittles?"

Pike walked back to the horse and untied the slicker-wrapped bundle lashed behind the cantle. He held it out to Vern, then began stripping the horse.

"This here is *beef*," Vern said as he opened the packet of meat. He cocked a suspicious eye toward Pike. "You ain't slaughtered one of *our* steers?"

There wasn't any answer.

"Boss ain't gonna like it."

"*I* wouldn't like going hungry," Pike muttered. "All the time we wasted hunting for you, we didn't have no chance to hunt game."

Vern felt obliged that they'd took the trouble to hunt for him. He couldn't rightly complain. And the half-smoked steaks Pike had begun to spear onto a sharp stick sure did smell like they'd cook up good. He owned to himself that there might be times when a man was justified in beefing a critter out of his own herd. He hoped it had been that damn golondrino that they'd butchered. That one wouldn't be missed much. It was a bunch-quitter and troublemaker to begin with.

Snuffy looked up from the fire, grinning guiltily. "We had to have *something* to eat, Vern. We rid off from the herd without nothing. No bedrolls, no cook pans, no coffee. We got to take what we can get."

Dutifully, Vern offered one more objection. But with the smell of the meat over the flames now, it was halfhearted. "We should have rounded up them beefs and got back to the herd like we was supposed to."

Pike snorted again. Shoving his hand into his pocket, he brought out the bandanna full of ore. "See that? That's just the beginning!"

Vern eyed it, suddenly awfully aware of having lost his own share, as well as his horse, his gun and most of his clothes. Replacing them would take quite a chunk out of his wage for the drive. There he'd be in Cheyenne, short of cash to begin with, while Pike and Snuffy were spending all that gold. A handful of ore — just one handful — would sure ease things. Maybe it wasn't such a bad idea to hunt around a bit more.

Maybe they'd stumble onto another cache. Just one handful . . . that was all he asked.

"All right," he mumbled, settling himself cross-legged on the ground. The heat of the fire was pleasantly warm where it glowed against his skin. But suddenly he felt the night cool chilling his bare back. It seemed almost as if he could feel the very darkness, up close behind him, like a cold breath on his spine.

Glancing around, he thought of that crazy old man again. "I don't much like making such an open camp."

"Why?" Snuffy asked.

"That hermit I told you about. Might be he'll come looking for us."

"Is there really an old man, Vern?"

"I told you so, didn't I?"

The kid leaned over the fire, squinting at the meat. It looked ready for eating. Taking the spit in one hand, he worked off a chunk with his knife, then handed the rest to Vern.

"You think I throwed away my horse and boots for fun?" Vern added, as he accepted the spit. He felt vaguely helpless without his own knife. Barehanded, he tugged at a steak, and passed the rest on to Pike.

"Yeah," Pike grunted. The way he saw it, Vern's story didn't make sense. How could, there be an old man living up here in the mountains? And if there was one, why would he act the way Vern claimed? Who would stake a feller out with rawhide that way? No, this was a windy Vern had dreamed up to scare them away from finding the gold. It wasn't gonna work, though.

"That old man don't want nobody else messing around in these mountains," Vern was saying. "If he comes prowling, he ain't gonna have no trouble at all finding us."

Pike eyed him suspiciously and asked, "What you think we ought to do about it?"

"Maybe post a night guard."

That might not be a bad idea, Pike told himself. Not because of any windy about a hermit, though. No, they ought to keep a close eye on Vern himself. Not give him a chance to go sneaking off in the dark.

"All right," he mumbled through a mouthful of meat. He swallowed and wiped at the grease on his face with his sleeve. "Snuff, how about you take first watch? You set till mid-dark. Then waken me and I'll set till dawn."

"I reckon I can take a turn," Vern offered.

"No, you're plumb beat up. You sleep. Me and Snuffy'll share the watch," Pike answered, feeling right pleased with his own cleverness."

Vern shrugged. He was willing to do his share of the work, but he wasn't gonna argue them for the privilege. Not when he ached so bad. He didn't fancy the idea of setting up a piece of the night, rubbing his eyes sore to keep them open.

Snuffy was agreeable to Pike's suggestion. He finished off his meat, scrubbed his hands against the thighs of his britches, and offered, "Vern, you take my saddle blanket. I'll trade with Pike when we change guard."

"Obliged," Vern muttered as he chawed at the last mouthful of meat. When he was done, he chose a spot up close to a boulder that would break the wind. Wrapping himself in Snuffy's blanket, he curled up. The scent of horse-sweat in the cloth was strong and familiar. Right homey. With a full belly, a blanket on his shoulders and soft ground under it, he felt a satisfied contentment. Might be there were things to worry about, like hunting gold and being hunted by some crazy old coot. But the worrying could all wait till morning. Almost as quickly as he closed his eyes he slept.

The old man had felt a salty yearning in his mouth as he sniffed at the night air. Them three'd built themselves a cook fire and had beef meat over it. Long time since he'd eaten from off a cow. Hell, he liked beef meat about as much as he did fresh young foal. Licking at his lips, he wondered how much of that meat they had. Maybe there'd be some left when he finished picking them off and had helped himself to their supplies.

He lay on his belly in the underbrush, peering at the shadows moving in the glimmer of their fire. It wasn't hard to tell the men apart. The medium-built one without a shirt was the towhead. One of the others was tall and skinny enough to squirm through a shotgun barrel. The third seemed to be a young'un not yet reached his growth. Listening to them talk, he sorted the voices. Even easier to tell 'em from the sounds they made than from their blurry images. The tall one made noises like he had a bone crossways in his gullet and was mad about it. The towhead spoke sort of soft and drawling. And the kid sounded like he was puzzled most of the time.

Kind of a shame to kill off a young lad like that, the old man thought. Still, the boy was old enough to know better than to try stealing another man's gold. A thief what would take something that wasn't rightly his deserved to die, no matter what his age. They all deserved to die.

He saw the towhead bed down, and in a moment the tall one followed. They left the kid to settle himself beside the fire, apparently keeping watch. He speculated on that, thinking as how it'd take a man with a mite of fox in him to lure away the kid without the others knew about it. Thing to do was get the boy off from the camp and kill him real quiet. Once that was done, he could sneak in and put his knife into the tall one. That'd leave the towhead who'd hexed his gun.

Using witch work against a man was downright unfair, the hermit thought. The towhead didn't deserve to die easy. Would have been rightful for him to have got pulled apart by that rawhide. Would be right to kill him slow and hard. L'arn him not to mess around with spells and hexes.

The old man wondered just what land of charm the towhead used. And whether another man might make use of it. Maybe he'd find out, before he finished off that witch.

On his belly, the rifle cradled in his arms, he began to squirm through the brush. First thing was to lure off the kid. He moved at an angle to the camp, heading toward the rabble of the landslide. The sounds he made were small, like the noises of night animals. He saw the kid at the fire glance in his direction, but casually, with no trace of suspicion.

Pausing, the old man searched over the ground with one hand. He found dry twigs. Taking one up between his fingers, he pressed gently. It snapped clean, a sharp sound in the night.

The kid looked startled. He scanned the darkness, his face vaguely wary now.

The old man moved a little further, skirting the edge of the landslide rubble, then stopped to snap another twig.

Snuffy got to his feet. It sure sounded like there was *something* creeping around out there. But suppose it was only an animal? Vern and Pike would have the laugh on him if he woke them up on account of some night critter. But if it wasn't an animal . . .

He drew the revolver from the holster at his hip. Against his suddenly sweaty palm it felt awkward and unhandy. He gripped it, trying hard to remember when he'd loaded it last and whether he'd fired it off during that stampede. He could recall doing a lot of hollering as he'd helped turn a bunch back into the main body of the herd. He remembered waving the pistol, thinking of firing it. But ammunition wasn't cheap. He hadn't wanted to waste it if he didn't have to. Now he couldn't recall whether he'd fired or not.

And maybe it was only some night critter making those noises in the brush.

He took a step away from the fire and squinted into the darkness. He'd been looking at the flame when he'd first heard the suspicious sounds. Now he realized that had been a mistake. All he could see was a dull mirage of the fire against a background of black. He blinked, trying to adjust his eyes. And cautiously he walked toward the last crackling of brash he'd heard.

The old man lay still, watching. The boy was coming over, real quiet, not disturbing the others. It was just what he'd wanted. Now he wanted that young'un to have reason to keep coming, right on across the open swath of rubble and into the far edge of the forest.

Still on his belly, he shinnied out of the bushes far enough to grab a handful of broken rock. He sent it skittering down the slope, a small clattering sound in the night. That should catch the kid's attention, he thought, grinning.

Tense as a fresh-looped colt, Snuffy started. He turned slowly, trying hard to see into the darkness. There were stars and a piece of a moon casting a thin light into the open, but the woods were stone black. Hesitantly, he moved on to the edge of the landslide path.

Suddenly he thought he saw something move. But as he jerked his head to look toward it, it was gone. Frowning, his hand locked tight on the butt of the gun, he headed for the place he thought he'd seen it.

Back in the deep shadows again, the old man set the butt of the rifle against the ground. Bracing against it, he hauled himself to his feet. Silently he cursed the stiffness in his knees. Funny how the night air would slack a bowstring, but tighten up a man's joints.

He leaned the gun against a tree and drew the wide-bladed knife from its sheath at his waist. His thumb tested its edge and he smiled with satisfaction. Crouching at the far side of the rock-strewn swath, he watched.

The kid paused a moment, then plunged on, his boots scraping the stone loud enough to waken a dead Injun. But it didn't seem to bother the two men sleeping back by the fire. The old man glimpsed one stirring slightly, then settling again.

He looked back toward the boy crossing over the open area. Just a little further, he thought. Just up to here . . .

As if answering a call, the kid kept coming. And then suddenly, with a scream like a shot wildcat, he disappeared.

The old man blinked. It was a trick of the night. The boy had been there one instant, backlit by the glow of the campfire. Then he was gone.

But a man couldn't disappear like that, he told himself as he rubbed at his watery eyes, then looked again. No, not unless it was more of the towhead's witch work.

Wheeling, he grabbed for the rifle and hurried back into the dark protection of the forest. When he paused to look over his shoulder, the barren swath of rubble was still empty. The kid was gone.

CHAPTER
SIX

It had that almost-human sound of a panther's scream. And it cut into Vern's sleep like a fresh-honed knife.

It'd spook the horses and maybe the beefs too, he thought as he sat up. He was half out of the blanket, groping for the boots that should have been at his side, when he realized he wasn't bedded with the herd.

And that wasn't a panther that had screamed.

"Sounds like Snuff!"

Vern jerked around at the words and saw Pike clambering out of his own blanket. His Colt's revolver was already in one hand.

Nodding agreement, Vern scrambled to his feet. Pike was up now, scanning the night. As the cry came again, he started up toward it.

Vern followed, feeling vaguely helpless without anything in his hands — not a rope nor gun nor even the reins of a horse. His fingers closed into fists as he lunged after Pike.

The scream faded. It left the night full of silence — a horribly complete silence. Not an animal grunted or chirruped or rustled the grass around them. That sharp, desperate cry had frozen the entire mountainside. But the silence didn't last long.

Vern felt a shiver run up his spine, as if rabbits were chasing over his grave. He wasn't sure which began first, the chill or that wail. It started low, then rose — a deep, hollow, muffled cry that seemed to come up from under the earth, as if it were some lost soul calling out from its coffin. And it shaped *his* name.

"Vern!"

An instant of silence, then, "Pike! Help!"

"That's Snuff," Vern whispered uncertainly. It kind of sounded like Snuffy, but there was sure something wrong with it. Why would the kid sound like he was hollering from somewhere under their feet?

"Help!"

"Yonder!" Pike swung up a still arm, pointing toward the expanse of landslide rubble.

It was too dark to see much out there. Vern squinted, but it didn't help. He could make out the forest across the way, and the rubble between him and it. But he couldn't see a sign of the kid.

He flexed his empty fingers. He needed a gun. Or a knife. Or something. To face a ghostly call like that, he needed light.

Striding back, he grabbed up a stick from the embers of the fire. He blew on it to rouse the flame, and hurried to Pike's side. Even with the torch, it took them a lot of hunting to find where the wailing voice was coming from.

It rose from a small ragged hole in the ground.

Hunkering, Vern let the firelight play along its edges. He could see as how a section of rock had dropped out, like a bung knocked into a barrel. But whatever was down there under the crust of stone was too deep for the torch's light to reach it.

"Vern? Pike? That you?" The voice came from the hole, still a plaintive wail, but sounding a lot more human now.

"You down there, Snuff?" Vern called back. He felt a real deep relief that it wasn't some haunt that had been hollering his name. Peering into the hole, he tried to shrug away the spooked feeling that lingered along his spine.

Pike was squatting at his side, staring into the hole too. Firelight glinted off the revolver he still held cocked. Vern glanced at it, glad for the assurance that Pike had been scared too.

"Yeah," Snuffy called back. "I've fell off something, Vern. I'm in a hole or a dry well or something. Can you get me out?"

"I reckon." Vern shifted the torch and bent his face down close to the opening, trying to see into it. A gust of cool, musty air played over his skin and licked at the flame. The light danced wildly, but it didn't reach to Snuffy.

"I can't see you," he called down. "If we lower a rope, can you get it? You ain't hurt or anything, are you?"

"I dunno." There was a pause. Then, thinly, "I can't stand up, Vern. I've twisted my knee or something. It hurts."

"Busted?"

"Don't think so. But I can't stand up on it! Help me, Vern!" The kid sounded as pitiful as an orphaned dogie. Awful lost and lonely.

80

"All right," Vern called down to him. Then he turned to Pike. "You fetch a throw rope. Better saddle a horse, too."

Rising, Pike nodded and headed back toward their camp.

Vern leaned over the opening again and hollered, "What you reckon you're in down there?"

"Dunno. Just a hole. Big one, though. I can't see nothing, just your fire up there. But I can hear water running. And I can *feel* it's big."

"Cave?"

"Reckon. It's awful dark down here. Where's that rope, Vern? You're gonna get me out, ain't you?"

"Sure. Pike'll be back with the rope in a minute."

"You got the makin's, Vern?"

His hand started for a shirt pocket. But he remembered he didn't have one. No tobacco, no shirt, nothing. He answered, "Sorry."

"Hell!" Snuffy hollered back.

"What's the matter?" Pike asked as he ambled up, leading his horse.

"He wants a smoke."

"He can have one when he gets up here."

"I want one, too."

Pike grunted and fumbled his nigh hand into a pocket. He brought out the Bull sack and handed it to Vern. Then he began uncoiling the rope he'd brought.

Vern set down the torch. He'd never got the hang of rolling one-handed. As he started to shake tobacco into the paper, his foot nudged the torch. The flame flickered, then disappeared, as the stick tumbled into the hole.

"What's that?" Snuffy screamed. "What's the matter!"

"Hell," Vern mumbled. He'd meant to take a light off that fire. And now he couldn't see what he was doing, either.

"What'd you do that for?" Pike asked.

"Didn't do it apurpose."

"Can't see what I'm doing," he grumbled. "And how's Snuffy gonna see the rope?"

"I don't reckon he could of seen it anyway," Vern said. "One of us better go down after him." He found wooden matches stuck in the band on the Bull sack and struck one.

"You better go," Pike told him.

"What's the matter up there?" Snuffy called again.

Vern gazed at the flame, waiting for the first shock of sulphur to burn away before he touched it to the cigarette. "Why me?"

"Why not?" Pike snapped back.

"I've done my share of climbing for the day."

"Hey, fellers!" Snuffy wailed from the darkness.

"Coming," Vern hollered down the hole. He feed up the quirly and took a deep drag.

Pike repeated, "*You* go down."

Vern started to answer him back, but didn't. Hell, Snuffy was down there, maybe hurt bad. Sure scared bad from the sound of it. This wasn't any time for the two of them to set up here arguing. *Somebody* had to go after the kid. He took another drag at the cigarette, then sighed and said, "All right. But I'm taking down your makin's."

"Go ahead." Pike got to his feet. Groping in the dark, he tied fast to the saddle horn and backed the horse away from the hole.

Vern tested the rope, then stuck a foot through the loop. He took the strings of the Bull sack between his teeth and began to lower himself gingerly into the hole. When the rope had his full weight, Pike started walking the horse slowly forward.

Vern rode the loop down into pitch-darkness, his free foot reaching for something solid. He didn't like this. He didn't like hanging in the air with nothing around him. And he didn't like being inside the ground at all. Man belonged in the open air, leastways as long as he was still alive. This seemed too much like being lowered into a grave. Except there likely hadn't ever been a grave dug this deep. It seemed like a hell of a long time before his foot finally found something under it.

"Ease off!" he hollered through his teeth as he touched ground.

"That you, Vern?" Snuffy called softly, sounding a little afraid of whatever it might be that had descended into the hole with him.

"Yeah." He felt the rope slacken and pulled his foot out of the loop. Then he took a match from the Bull sack and struck it. The fumes filled his nose, and the flamelight groped into a darkness it couldn't begin to fill.

Snuffy was almost under his feet, propped up on one elbow and blinking at him.

With a sigh of relief, the kid stammered, "I — I sure am glad to see you."

"Here." Vern tossed him the makings. The kid caught the sack, fumbled and dropped it.

Bending slow, so as not to let the match he held go out, Vern picked up the dead torch. He played the light along the burnt end and in a moment it caught, rousing into a far larger flame than the match had held. That was a lot better. He held it out while Snuffy retrieved the Bull sack and fingered together a smoke. Then he stood up and turned slowly, looking around.

Snuffy had been right. The cave was a big one. The roof overhead was a ragged dome of rock, sloping into deep shadows and sharp outjuts of stone wall. It all looked water-worn, like a riverbed canyon had been flopped over, upside-down on the ground.

The dome and walls were rough, but the ground underfoot was surprisingly even. There were a few upthrusts of rock, and some heaps of big slabs that seemed to have fallen from the roof. But in between, there was gravel that seemed almost to have been spread and packed for footing.

Hunkering, Vern scooped up a fistful of the gravel and put the light close to it. There were chips of white rock mixed in with the brown and gray. Real shiny white stone just like the stuff that Spanish gold had been bedded in.

"What's going on down there?" Pike called from above.

"Just looking around," Vern answered.

Snuffy put the quirly to his mouth, drew a long lungful of smoke, and let it out again. "Let's us get out of here, huh?"

"You in pain?" Vern asked him.

"No. Don't reckon so."

"Then hold on a minute. I want to do some more looking."

"What's the matter?"

"See this?" Vern held the handful of gravel toward him.

He poked at it with a forefinger. "Rock."

"Look familiar?"

"I dunno. Rock's rock, ain't it?" He took a pinch of gravel between his fingers, squinted at it close, then, shrugged.

"Just lemme look some more," Vern said, standing again. He began to move toward the walls, holding up the torch. In one direction there were a mess of big slabs of stone, making a jumbled barrier that completely closed off that end of the cave. Turning, he walked the length of the chamber. There were more slabs at the other end, but they didn't block the way altogether. Scrambling up, he held out the torch and leaned over. The dome echoed his sudden sharp intake of breath.

"What's the matter?" Snuffy called.

"We got us another dead Spaniard," Vern answered in a harsh whisper. He stared at the skeleton lying beyond the heap of slabs.

This one wasn't busted up. It was stretched out in the form of a man. There was another Spanish hat and breastplate, too, but they weren't mixed with the bones.

Instead, they lay to one side, as if the Spaniard had stripped himself of them before he died.

Vern stepped over the slab and bent down. Tentatively, he touched the breastplate. It fell into flakes of damp-rotten rust. A rust-covered thing nearby looked like it might have been a weapon of some sort. Not exactly a tomahawk, but something in that line. Only a lot bigger. He started to reach for it, then changed his mind. That was the dead man's weapon.

He glanced at other rusted objects, then looked up at the walls. The surface was covered with scratches and gouges. Pick marks. It had been worked over. Only a few traces of white stone still clung to the dark wall rock.

As he started to turn back toward Snuffy with news of his find, he spotted the pile of lumps along the far wall. And he realized they weren't rounded stones heaped up there. Anxious with his own thoughts, but moving cautiously, he stepped over the skeleton and headed toward them.

"What you up to, Vern?" Snuffy called impatiently.

"Just a minute!" he hollered back, his voice thin with excitement. He held the torch close over the lumps. They were leather pokes, all stacked up neat and even. And all old as hell. The one he prodded fell apart at this touch. It spilled out shards of that white rock, all glimmering with metallic yellow. Just like the ore they'd found with the other dead Spaniard.

He gazed at the gold that glinted under his torchlight and drew a deep breath that went down his throat in a lump. Softly, not quite believing his eyes, he said, "We found it."

"What?" Snuffy hollered. He'd heard the voice but hadn't been able to make out the words.

Vern grabbed up a handful of the ore. And this time he shouted. He leaned back his head and hollered with joy. "We found it!"

His voice echoed, rumbling like distant thunder across the dome and back again. He wheeled, jumping over the skeleton and scrambling across the slabs of rock. Dropping to his knees at Snuffy's side, he opened his hand and repeated, "We found it!"

"What the hell is going on down there?" Pike shouted from above.

Snuffy looked toward the hole and called back, "Vern's found the gold!"

"*What!*"

"The gold!" Vern hollered. "This here cave Snuffy busted into — it's the Spanish mine we been looking for! It's full of the stuff!"

Pike stared in silence. He hunkered at the edge of the opening, gazing down at the two figures dimlit by the torch Vern held. The words registered themselves in his mind. He whispered, "Gold . . ."

Slowly he rose to his feet. He stretched out his arms as if he could reach from one end of the world to the other. And he began to jig. Bouncing up and down in wild delight, he sang it to himself over and over, "Gold, gold, gold . . ."

The world was *his. All his!*

He stopped jouncing and drew a deep breath. No, not quite all his. It was Vern's and Snuffy's too. *Vern's?* Dammit, Vern had known all the time that the mine was down there. Now he was playacting, making out he'd just found it so as to trick them out of believing he had meant to keep it all for himself.

The wide grin faded off his face. He hunkered again, peering with suspicion at Vern's shadowy figure.

Snuffy cupped both hands and Vern poured the fist full of gold into them.

"There's more," he told the kid, his voice soft with awe at the thought. "There's a whole heap of pokes, all full of it. Looks like them Spaniards cleaned out the lode for us. They mined it out and stacked it up all neat and just ready for us to take it."

The boy stared at the ore in his hands and beamed.

"It is ours, ain't it, Vern?"

"Sure." Vern gazed at visions in his own mind. Handtooled boots, a fancy riding horse, a good hat. Hell, all that and maybe a spread of his own besides. He shook his head slowly, wondering if he might be dreaming all this. Maybe he'd waken rolled in Snuffy's blanket and dead broke without his boots again. It was awful hard to believe *he* could find a gold mine. But that ore sure looked real.

The Bull sack lay at Snuffy's side. Vern reached for it with a hand that shook so hard he could hardly grab it up. He thrust the torch toward the kid. "Hold this."

Snuffy took it and watched as Vern struggled together a misshapen smoke. Vern finally got the thing made and lit. Sitting back on his haunches, he looked into Snuffy's face. His hand groped automatically to push the Bull sack into a breast pocket he discovered he didn't have.

Grinning, he said, "First thing I'm gonna buy me is a new shirt."

The old man squatted at the side of a tree, his arm brushing its trunk, as he looked out across the landslide rubble. His eyes might not be too sharp, but they weren't *that* bad. He knew he'd seen the kid right out there one moment, and *not* there the next. But he could sure hear him bellering from somewhere nearby.

The movements in camp took his attention. He could make out the other two scrambling from their blankets and running into the open. The tall one first, with a gun in his hand. The towhead followed, then stepped back to grab up a torch.

The old man's face pinched up with the effort of trying to make out their words. Some of what they said was too soft-spoken for him to catch. But what they hollered down the hole in the ground came to him clear enough, and he realized what had happened to the boy.

It wasn't the towhead's hex working after all, he told himself, relieved. It was simply that the young one had fell into a sink hole. He was glad of that. For a moment there, he'd been right worried about the workings of the hex charm.

He saw one of them fetch a horse, then the other slump down a rope, disappearing into the earth. Watching curiously, he felt nigh as impatient as the one who waited above.

89

A voice, high-pitched and excited, rattled up out of the ground. It was muffled, all blurred by echoes. But the old man's ears caught the words.

We found gold!

He rocked back on his heels as if he'd been slapped in the face. They had found it. They'd found his gold!

Anger surged up from his gut, burning in his throat. All the years he had hunted these hills, and now those three sneak thieves had just plain stumbled onto *his* gold.

His thumb grabbed at the hammer of the rifle. But the gun wobbled in his hands as he lifted it to his shoulder. Over the blurring sights, he saw the man at the edge of the hole rise and begin to jog up and down, waving his arms frantically.

For a moment the old man was puzzled. Then he understood and grinned. He could feel the excitement of it himself, creeping through his bones. It burned in him, just as if it were he who had found the lode.

Hell, it was *his* goldl Now it was found, all he had to do was take possession of it. He felt like dancing around some himself. But nobody with the sense of a last year's bird nest would have done a fool thing like that.

Setting back on his heels, he lowered the gun and stroked it as if it were something alive that could share his feelings. And he pondered that hole.

He'd gone over this ground more times than a man had fingers to count on. Over and over again, he'd followed the trail the Spanish markers pointed, always ending up here, looking for just one more mark, or whatever the arrows had pointed to. He'd seen for himself how there'd been a landslide sometime back. He'd searched through the nibble all the way down as far as it went, looking for a marker stone that might have rolled with it. He'd never found a thing, though. There hadn't been any holes in the ground then. Hadn't been a single sign of a cave or a mine.

It was the towhead's witch work that had opened the hole, he decided. Likely the landslide had blocked off the mine's original entrance, covering every trace of it. Wouldn't never anybody have found it without he had some kind of charm working for him.

That towhead's trick was right handy. He wondered what kind of charm it was. He could sure use a power like that himself. Petting the gun, he wondered if he might be able to take the towhead alive and get the secret out of him. He knew a lot of Injun ways. For sure some one of them would make that man-witch talk.

Out there by the hole, the tall one was backing the horse, hauling up the rope. The other two both rode it up. They scrambled out of the hole, sprawling on the ground, and began to talk excitedly among themselves.

They were all too excited to hold their voices low. The old man could hear what they were saying to each other easily enough this time. Intrigued, he listened to the towhead's story. He grinned to himself again as the feller finished off: ". . . already mined and packed. Just waiting for us to haul it out and take it off!"

That put a new thought into the hermit's head. He considered it as he listened.

The young one whispered, "Gee-zus!" He sounded every bit as surprised as if he hadn't been down there himself. The three of them went on talking, deciding there wasn't much to be done now in the dark. Come morning they'd fetch over the horses and start bringing up the ore. From what the towhead told them, the two mounts could pack it all, though it'd make quite a load.

The plans took shape in the old man's head. He'd just set here and let them boys do the heavy work. No point in him straining his old bones when he had such willing help. He'd let them bring up the gold and load it onto the horses. Then he'd get rid of the three of them and take the animals. Easy enough. Just fine!

CHAPTER
SEVEN

Snuffy's knee was only twisted. By morning he was able to walk all right, even if he did limp and grunt a mite. He gave Vern a hand letting Pike down the rope to look over the cave. Then Pike came up and they worked out their plans for bringing out the ore.

It was Vern who got elected to go down and handle it inside the cave. He tried objecting, but Pike said as how Snuffy couldn't do it with his banged-up leg, and he himself had to stay up top to raise and lower the rope.

"*I* can lift the rope up and down," Vern answered. He didn't much want to work in the cave. Something about being inside a hole in the ground just didn't set well with him. It gave him an unpleasant feeling along the backbone. But Pike was adamant, so finally Vern gave in and rode the rope down again.

He took down wood and matches, so at the bottom he was able to get a fire going. It cast a fair amount of light, and that helped ease his unhappy feelings. Resigning himself he rigged a sling out of the slicker Pike tossed down, and started loading on the gold.

He found that if he handled them carefully, most of those old leather sacks could be moved without they fell apart in his hands. A few did bust open. He scooped up every speck of the spilled ore, dumping it into the sling too. All in all, it took quite a while and a lot of work. But he had plenty of time to rest between loads as Pike hauled up the sling and emptied it out.

The sun crept up higher and higher, pouring its light through the hole overhead in a sharp-edged shaft. Vern judged it must be nigh onto noon when he finally heaved the last of the ore onto the slicker and hollered for Pike to haul away. He settled himself on a slab of rock and watched the bundle rise up, then disappear over the edge. The hole showed a bright ragged patch of real blue sky. He gazed at it, anxious to be up top again.

Even with so much sunlight spilling into the cave now, he didn't like being here. He didn't like the musty damp smell or the funny way little breezes worked around, brushing against his face and bare shoulders like the whispery touch of something unseen. He didn't like thinking about that skeleton lying behind the rocks where he'd had to step over it every time he'd gone in or out after the ore. It had seemed almost like it was staring at him with its empty eyeholes, and grinning like it knew things. Evil things.

Pike was sure taking his time, he thought as he watched the empty hole. It seemed like he should have got the sling loose and the rope started back down by now. Leaning back his head, he hollered, "Hey, Pike!"

The answer came back as from a distance, "Hold yer water, dammit!"

He shrugged, telling himself he must be rushing time in his mind. He couldn't have been waiting as long as he felt like he had. And worrying over it just made the time drag slower. He put himself to thinking about what he'd do with his share of that gold.

It was still hard to believe all this was real, even though he'd handled all the ore himself. Loads of it — plenty enough for a spread of his own and a string of fine riding horses, fancy Mex boots and a new Stetson, spurs with silver janglebobs, and folks calling him *Mister* . . .

Grinning at his own thoughts, he looked toward that hole overhead. It was still empty. Where the hell was that rope?

"Pike!" he called.

This time there wasn't any answer.

He shouted again. His voice echoed within the cave, filling the shadows with spooks that whispered his words back at him in mockery. A shiver ran up his spine. As the echoed died, he caught faint sounds from above. Iron shoes clattered over rubble as two horses began to walk slowly. Heading away . . .

"Pike!" He screamed, suddenly cold all over. "Pike! Snuffy!"

The sounds of hooves faded and were gone. And he knew that Pike and Snuffy were gone too.

The old man had wakened as soon as the intruders began to stir in their camp that morning. From his hiding place in the brush, he'd watched them make their preparations and begin to bring the ore up from, the mine. He'd grinned to himself as they'd made two bundles of their slickers and lashed them onto the horses' rumps. Right kind of them to do all that hard work for him.

With amazement, he watched the two of them mount up and start off. They'd left the towhead down in that hole!

Whatever the hex that one was using, it sure didn't seem to be working for him now. Leastways not against his double-crossing pardners. Even so, the old man wanted that charm. He wanted the towhead alive and able to talk.

He considered a moment. The cave seemed like a good safe place to leave the towhead wait while he took care of his business with the other two sneak thieves. Then he could come back and find out about that witch hex at his leisure.

The two horsemen were out of sight. Rising from his hiding place, the old man started after them. He ambled along happily. The heavy-laden horses made good clear marks where they trod. Their trail was easy enough that a spanking-bare papoose could have followed it blindfolded.

They couldn't travel fast or far with their horses loaded down that way, he figured. Should have walked and led their pack animals, the way he'd done when he was young. He shook his head as he thought about it. Fool young'uns these days didn't have no spunk or sense. They weren't nothing like men had been back in his day. Feller had to live by his wits back then. These two didn't have the sense of a jaybird between them. Young'uns these days were going to hell in a bucket.

He grinned again, thinking as how a sly old fox like himself could outwit a pair like that twice a day and end over end on Sundays. He'd just follow along till they'd wore out the horses and stopped to rest. Then he'd pick off one after the other. He'd claim his gold and the horses, then head back and collect the man-witch from out the cave. All real simple and easy for a feller with his wits about him. Yes sir!

Snuffy had stood by, holding the horse, as Pike emptied out the sling. It wasn't till the third load came up that he asked, "Why you only making two heaps of that stuff? There's *three* of us."

"There's only *two* horses," Pike had answered, not even bothering to look up at him.

He'd been right quiet for a while after that. Pike had a way of talking that made him feel awful dumb. Lot of fellers talked to him that way. Vern hardly ever did, though. That was one reason he liked Vern.

He watched a ground squirrel poke its nose out of the brush. It stared back at him for a brief moment, then disappeared again. Overhead a hawk wheeled in its search for game. The sky beyond it was clear and brilliant.

Snuffy liked it here in the mountains. All the strange funny scents in the air caught his fancy. He wished he had the time to poke around in the woods and see the things that were so different here from back home. He sure did admire all the cricks full of such sweet water. It'd be fun to lay hid near one of them and watch the critters come down to drink. Man might even make friends with some of them, if he was gentle and careful and didn't spook 'em, he figured. Once he'd cashed in his share of all that gold, might be he'd come back here and camp out a while. Not a hunting trip, though. He didn't much care for hunting except just enough to keep himself fed. He didn't like killing things.

Frowning, he wondered why Pike was unknotting the rope from the slicker and coiling it. Vern was still down in the cave. What was Pike putting the rope up for? He started to ask, then stopped himself. There was some good reason, else Pike wouldn't be doing it. And Pike would give him an answer that would make him feel like a fool again.

"Gimme a hand here," Pike said.

Obediently, Snuffy limped over and helped him heft up one of the slicker-wrapped bundles of ore. Together they heaved it behind the cantle of Pike's saddle. Snuffy braced it there while Pike lashed it in place with the tie strings.

When the second bundle had been tied firm behind Snuffy's saddle, Pike said, "Mount up and let's get going."

Snuffy stared at him, then looked back toward the hole in the ground. Foolish or not, he was going to ask the question in his mind this time. "What about Vern?"

"What about him?" Pike snapped.

But Snuffy wasn't giving in to that tone of voice this time. He felt real certain something was wrong. Leastways, he wanted to understand what Pike was doing. He protested, "He's still down in the cave. He can't get out without the rope. We ain't gonna leave him there, are we?"

Pike grunted.

"But . . ."

"Shut up and get on your horse!"

Snuffy winced as if he'd been slapped. But he stood his ground. "No! What you want to go off and leave Vern for?"

Pike's mouth worked, except that no words came out. He looked dark and fierce, real angry. Then he sighed and said, "Look here, boy. Vern tried to bluff us and edge us out of our share of the gold, didn't he?"

Slowly Snuffy nodded. He guessed that was so. From what Pike had said, it sure looked that way. And Pike had sounded like he knew what he was talking about.

"Well, Vern deserves a lesson, don't he?"

He nodded again, not at all sure what Pike was getting at.

Pike gazed at the kid feeling tempted to slap him down. Why did the damnfool have to up and get balky now? Well, he didn't mean to let Snuffy cause him any trouble. And he sure wasn't going to share part of that gold with Vern.

He'd been considering it half the night, and again this morning. He'd weighed it back and forth in his mind, asking himself why Vern should get a share after the way he'd tried to steal it all. He'd repeated it to himself, getting madder and madder, until he'd hated Vern with all his gut.

Once that was established and he'd convinced himself that Vern was a no-good son the world would be better off without, he'd been able to enjoy making his plans. Vern had to be the one who went down into the mine. And once Vern got down there, he wasn't ever coming out again.

Studying Snuffy's face, Pike realized he couldn't tell the kid that. Snuff was too dumb to understand, and too softhearted to go along with the idea. The kid didn't appreciate having a treasure, dropped into his lap. He'd be willing to share with Vern, no matter what.

Holding tight rein on his temper, Pike pondered some answer that would satisfy Snuffy and get him moving. In as soft and coaxing a voice as he could muster, he said, "It's all right, boy. We ain't hurting ol' Vern, are we? He can take care of himself, can't he?"

Again Snuffy nodded uncertainly.

"All he's got to do is climb out that hole and follow along. He'll get back to the herd all right. And when we see him again, we'll all have a good laugh about it, won't we?"

"Are you sure he can get out without you let a rope down to him?"

"Yeah," Pike grunted as he rose to his saddle. "I looked that cave over good. It'll be a piece of work for him, but he can do it." His back was to the kid. He didn't want to chance Snuffy seeing in his face that he was lying. Sure, he'd looked the cave over good. He'd made real certain that a man couldn't climb up to that hole in its roof without a rope. Vern was as good as buried down there.

Reluctantly Snuffy swung up onto the bay. He didn't like it, but Pike said that it was all right. And Pike sounded like he knew what he was talking about. Snuffy allowed to himself that whenever he had a disagreement with anybody, the other feller usually turned out to be right. Leastways, the other feller usually won the arguing, and that was the same thing, wasn't it?

In obedient silence, he gigged his horse and followed Pike on into the forest.

Nagging thoughts edged Pike's mind as he rode. Leaving Vern trapped in the cave was murder. Or was it? He answered the thin thread of conscience. No! Vern was no better than a thief. He didn't deserve a share of the gold. Or a chance to get away. All a thief deserved was killing. It was only just to leave Vern to die.

And the gold would sure divvy up nicer into two shares than three. Any sensible man could see that. Pike counted himself a damned sensible man.

Reaching back, he patted the bundle behind his saddle. What was done to Vern was only fair, he told himself. After all, it was what Vern would have done to him if things had been the other way around, wasn't it? And he had more important problems to concern himself with. He had to plan for the future.

The small voice of conscience had been weak to begin with. Stifling it, he turned his thoughts to rejoining the trail herd. That would be a damnfool thing to do. The other hands would for sure get wind of his treasure. Best thing would be to stay in the high country, paralleling the cattle trail. He and Snuffy could travel fast enough to pass the herd. They could reach Cheyenne and be on board a train to someplace else before the Boss arrived in town and found out they'd been there.

He thought about San Francisco. That seemed like a real fine place to go. From what he'd heard it was one helluva town. A man could flash around a poke full of raw ore there without he roused any suspicions. Yeah, he'd head for San Francisco. He didn't doubt he could make Snuffy go along with the plan.

As he glanced back toward the boy, Snuffy called out to him, "I'm hungry."

Anger flared in Pike. The kid had already said that at least half a dozen times in the past couple of hours. It was beginning to wear at his nerves.

His horse stumbled. It jerked, recovering its balance, and Pike spat out an angry word as he tugged sharply at the reins. It seemed like everything was working against him. The kid kept hollering about food, the horses were lagging along, dragging their feet, and now it felt like that sudden jolt had loosened the bundle behind his saddle.

Yeah, one of the tie strings had slipped and was coming loose. With a long, weary sigh of disgust, he called back to the kid, "All right. Once we're over this next ridge, we'll stop and eat."

Snuffy grinned, and that annoyed him, too. It was a damned stupid grin, as far as he was concerned. The boy was an idiot who didn't deserve having a treasure dumped into his lap.

The far side of the ridge sloped into a shallow gully with a trickle of water running through it. The game trail widened at the water's edge. Pike drew rein there and slid out of the saddle.

"Ne'mind the horses. Just let 'em drink," he told Snuffy, "We ain't gonna stop any longer than it takes to get your belly full and your mouth shut."

Nodding, the boy stepped out of the saddle and began to gather firewood. By the time Pike had finished remaking and snugging down the bundle of gold, he had the fire going and the meat over it.

The scent of cooking tickled Pike's nose. Reluctantly he admitted to himself that he was hungry too. As he seated himself on the ground beside Snuffy, he grumbled, "Hope you got enough cooking there for both of us."

The kidd nodded.

And something exploded.

Pike jumped at the sound of the rifle shot. Vaulting to his feet, he stood as if frozen, his thoughts too broken and churning to give him direction.

Eyes wide and startled, Snuffy looked up. His hands groped, then pressed against his chest.

Pike glimpsed the stain of red beginning to blossom on the kid's shirt as the spread fingers touched it. He saw Snuffy lean forward. Making a small gurgling noise, the kid folded into a heap at the side of the fire.

Pike's trance broke. He lunged toward the horses. His right hand grabbed for the Colt at his thigh as the left reached for his mount's reins.

Ducking for cover behind the horse, he flung one wild shot into the brash.

At the blast of the gun, the horse snorted. Its nostrils flared at the stench of powdersmoke so close to its face. Jerking at the reins Pike held, it danced nervously.

He grabbed at the horn and slung himself up into the saddle. Hitting leather, he threw another shot into the brush.

He was answered in lead. A slug skimmed close past his head, buzzing like an insane bee. He seemed to feel the breeze of it on the back of his neck, an icy wind that sent a chill shuddering the length of his spine.

His spurs jabbed viciously into the horse's flanks, drawing a snort of pain. With a frantic toss of its head, the animal broke into a wild gallop.

The shooting had startled Snuffy's bay. It stood with its head high and its hooves shuffling, uncertain whether to obey the dragging reins that held it ground-hitched, or to break and run. Taking a tentative step, it put a hoof on a rein end. The sharp jerk of the bit halted it.

Pike was across the gully, clambering his mount up the far slope toward the trees when he glanced back. He saw Snuffy up on his knees. The kid's voice came in a thin, wavering scream, "Pike! Help me!"

Leaning low over the pommel, Pike raked his spurs along his mount's sides, driving it on into the woods. *To hell with the damnfool kid!* He turned his attention ahead. The low branches were whipping at him. He bent himself down further until the saddle horn was pressed hard into his belly.

A third shot sounded behind him. He glanced back again. He couldn't spot any sign of the hidden sniper.

But he saw Snuffy up on his feet, clinging to a stirrup and trying desperately to drag himself onto the excited bay.

The kid caught at the saddle and somehow managed to haul himself onto it. As he struggled a leg over the cantle, his boot nudged the slicker-wrapped bundle tied there.

Pike remembered the gold. With a hard jab of the bit, he wheeled his mount. He knew he was lunging back into range of the hidden rifle. But, dammit, he *couldn't* leave all that gold behind. Hell no!

Swinging his horse, he grabbed for Snuffy's reins. As he caught them, the kid let go and grappled his fingers into the bay's mane. His eyes on Pike were moist and grateful.

Pike slammed with his spurs again, panicking his mount into another desperate run. And the bay, bad scared, scrambled to keep up.

He didn't ease the pace until he was deep into the woods. When he finally slowed and looked back, he knew he'd put a lot of ground between himself and whoever had been doing that shooting. It was safe to take it easy for a while now.

He glanced at Snuffy. The kid sprawled across the saddle bow, one hand still wrapped in the bay's mane. The other hung down its withers, limp fingers red-stained and dripping. The back of his shirt fluttered slightly with his shallow-drawn breaths.

Pike grunted with disgust. It was the lad's share of the gold he'd risked his neck riding back for. He felt a moment of regret that Snuffy hadn't fallen off or died or something. A prick of conscience rose to stifle the thought, but remnants of it lingered at the edge of his mind as he rode on, leading the bay.

CHAPTER
EIGHT

Vern gave up shouting. He'd made as much noise as he could and he'd gotten no answer. He was convinced now that nobody was close enough to hear him — or else nobody was willing to pay him any attention. He was just making his throat raw and wasting his breath trying to call them back.

They'd damn well *meant to* go off and leave him in this hole.

What would they do a thing like that for? He couldn't understand it. He'd known all along that Pike had a kind of ornery streak, but he'd never thought Pike was mean enough to do something like this. And Snuffy sure wasn't the kind who'd abandon a man all alone in a hole in the middle of nowhere. But whether it made sense or not, they'd done it to him.

Damn them! They hadn't no call to pull a trick like this on him. He was sure going to give them hell when he got out.

If he got out . . .

The thought was sudden. And it ran like ice through his veins. There might not be any way out.

"The hell," he muttered aloud. Bedamned if he'd even think such a thing. There *was* some way out and he'd find it. No miserable cold hole in the ground was going to claim *his* bones. Not like thisl

Picking up a stick from the fire, he started to examine the cave's walls. The stone was seamed with thin cracks and narrow fissures. From somewhere behind it, he could hear the muffled sound of fast-flowing water. He caught scents of it in the odd, twisting little air currents that squirmed around him.

Scrambling onto a heap of fallen rock, he peered into a hole too deep for his torchlight to penetrate its darkness. The smell of water was strong in it. He reached into explore with his fingers, but found only cold, damp stone.

As he climbed down the rocks, a new play of air touched his face. He stopped, poised like a hound. There was more than just the scent of water in that breeze.

It was a man-smell, like the odor that hung over a campsite that had been in use for a long while — a mixed smell of wastes, old cook fires and stale tobacco smoke.

The scents were faint, more like echoes than anything real. A ghost of the old Spanish camp tantalizing him?

Cautiously, as if he were afraid of scaring away the smells, he moved the torch, watching the flicker of the flame. There was an air current. It came from the crack between the cave's wall and a huge leaning slab of stone propped against it.

Pressing his face to the crack, he caught a strong enough whiff of the man-scent to convince himself it was no ghost. There *was* a campsite somewhere at the other end of that crack. So there had to be an opening to the cave off that way.

He hollered into the crack.

His voice came back to him in a wailing, shuddering echo. It was the only answer.

He tried shoving his hand into the hole. It was barely wide enough to let him squeeze through his knuckles. He couldn't force it in past the heel of his palm. And for a horrible frightful moment he was afraid he couldn't haul it back out again either.

But then it slid free. Sucking at his scraped knuckles, he told himself he had to be a mite more careful. Things were bad enough right now. If he up and got his hand stuck in a hole like that, even a ladder wouldn't get him out of this mess.

That crack between the slab and the wall wasn't big enough to do him much good. But what kind of opening was behind the slab, he wondered. He shoved, at it with one hand, then both. It felt as solid as the mountain itself. Leaning his shoulder, he braced his feet and put his full strength against it. Not a budge. He'd need a prybar to heft a slab like that. And he didn't have any tools at all. Or did he?

He recalled the rusty axhead thing lying by the Spaniard's skeleton. It wasn't any prybar, but it might be useful. He sure didn't have anything to lose by trying it.

When he struck it against a rock flakes of rust shattered away from, its surface. But the iron underneath was sound. And it was a thick-butted wedge. He forced the narrow end into the crack between the slab and the wall, then turned to hunt for a good-sized piece of stone to hammer with.

The first couple of blows only sent more flakes of rust flying. But then he felt the wedge move. Gingerly, he tested the width of the crack. His knuckles slid in easily now. Picking up the hammer stone in both hands, he flung all of his strength behind the next blow.

With a screeching, the wedge drove deeper. The huge slab of stone had visibly shifted.

Vern could feel his heart banging against his ribs. Sweat trickled down his face. He wiped at it, then leaned back and heaved the hammer stone again.

The slab poised, trembling like a nervous horse. Instinctively, he leaped back from it. With a deep, creaking groan, it swayed forward. And fell.

The earth under his feet winced with the impact. Thunder cracked in the chamber, echoing and reechoing in a rolling roar. As the slab struck, it spewed dust and chips of busted rock.

Crouching with his arms flung up in front of his face, Vern felt as if he'd been caught in the middle of a powder blast. Flying rock shards stung at his bare skin. The echoes pounded his ears. It seemed like all hell had broke loose.

The bits of rock fell to the earth. But the dust hung heavy in the air, and the thunder still rung inside his head as he lowered his arms to squint at the fallen slab. He had a strong feeling a man could get hurt messing around knocking down things like that. For a minute there he'd been afraid he'd tore loose the roots of the mountain and the whole thing was gonna tumble in on him.

Looking up at the wall of the cave he'd bared, he let out a whoop of joy. There was a hole in it all right. One plenty big enough for a man to squeeze himself into. And the wind gusted through it now, filled with the camp scent.

His torch was gone. He hurried to fetch another one and thrust it as far as he could into the hole. The flame flickered in the breeze, showing him a few feet of narrow tunnel and then darkness.

For a moment he considered the possibilities. That crawlhole might turn too small for a man to get through. It might not lead anywhere after all. The whole damned mountain might fall in on him. Hell any number of things could go wrong. But what alternative was there?

The air currents told him there was an opening somewhere up that passage. And he *had* to find a way out. Shrugging, he wiped his hands on his thighs. He had to *try*.

Hoisting himself up, he squirmed head first into the fissure. As he reached for the torch, it went out. The darkness that closed over him was blacker than any he'd ever imagined. He hesitated, thinking of backing out and fetching another one. But it would probably die too.

With a sigh of determination, he dug in his elbows and shoved himself deeper into the cramped gut of the mountain.

★ ★ ★

110

The horse stumbled again. And Pike cursed it again, jabbing hard at its jaw with the bit. It didn't help. Laden with the weight of the man and gold, pushed at a pace too fast, the beast was weary beyond responding to the pain. And Pike knew it.

He couldn't admit to himself that he was scared, so he was angry instead. Mad as hell at everything and everybody, except himself. He mumbled his curses through clenched teeth.

The bay at his flank staggered against his mount. Foam flagging from its mouth spattered on his leg. He twisted in the saddle, slapping at the bay's face.

As it tossed up its head to evade the blow, the boy clinging to its back struggled to look up. "Pike," he called hoarsely. "Pike, I gotta rest."

Pike studied the woods behind the kid. Somewhere back there, someone was stalking him with a rifle. He was sure of that. But he had pushed the horses across a good piece of land since those shots had been fired, and he knew he couldn't push them much further. Not without they both gave out on him. He couldn't let that happen. He needed the horses to haul the gold.

"All right," he grumbled. Halting, he surveyed the land around him. At first he thought it would be best to go deeper into the woods and hide in the underbrush. But then it came to him that the boulder-strewn meadow ahead would be better. One of those massive clusters of rock would offer cover, and nobody'd be able to sneak up across the open area around it.

He jabbed his spurs into the horse's sides, urging it into a shambling walk, and tugged at the bay's reins.

"Pike!" Snuffy called desperately.

"Just a minute more," he snapped back. It was all Snuffy's fault, he told himself. If the damned kid hadn't insisted on stopping to eat, none of this would have happened. Everything had been going fine up until then.

He found a niche in one jumbled heap of rock that would provide protection from two sides, and drew rein again.

As his feet touched ground, he gave out a deep grunt. It was tension, more than the hard ride, that had his muscles strung out, feeling like a thousand pinpoints of pain were thrust into them. He was still tense. His hands almost trembled as he tugged out his Bull sack and began to build a smoke.

"Pike?" Snuffy called plaintively. He was hanging lop-sidedly to the saddle, about to slide out of it. Roughly, Pike helped him to the ground.

Snuffy lay motionless, but for the shuddering of his chest as he sucked breath. The whole front of his shirt was dark-stained.

Settling on his rump Pike lit his quirly and looked at the kid. He wondered just how bad Snuffy was hurt. From the gurgling sounds he made breathing, and the paleness of his face, the boy was in pretty bad shape. Well, it was his own damn fault, Pike repeated to himself.

Through half-open eyes, Snuffy gazed at the scarecrow figure seated on the rocks. He felt as if he were drifting along the edges of sleep, uncertain what was a dream and what was real. He hoped Pike was real. He had a notion he needed help. There was an awful cramped feeling in his chest, like something was cinched tight around it. Every time he took a breath, there was a sharp dart of pain. But even that seemed like something from a dream.

A hazy memory flickered into his mind. He concentrated, bringing it into focus. Somebody had shot him. That seemed awful strange. He wondered why it had happened. Who'd want to do a thing like that to him?

Scraping up a voice that sounded like dry gravel he forced out words. "Pike, who shot me?"

With a jerk of head, Pike snarled, "Who the hell do you think? Vern!"

"Huh?"

"Had to be Vern," he continued, talking to himself more than to the kid. "Who else could it have been? Who else knows we got that gold? He was lying to us about that mine. He knew some other way into it. He's got himself out and got hold of a gun. Now he's stalking us."

"What — what did he want to shoot me for?"

"He wants the gold. Wants all of it for himself. Hell kill us both and steal it, if we give him the chance." As he said it, Pike scanned the edge of the woods.

It had been a mistake not to put a bullet into Vern, he thought. He was certain he knew exactly what Vern had in mind — it was what *he'd* do in the same spot. Sure, if it was Vern and the kid who'd got the gold and run off from him, *he'd* track them down and kill them both.

Gazing at the sky around the lowering sun, he thought as how it'd be a clear night. Lots of stars and a fair piece of moon to give light. A good night for a hunter — only maybe the quarry would turn hunter this night. Maybe Vern would be in for a real surprise when he came creeping through the night, meaning to kill.

The tension in Pike was easing as a plan took shape in his mind. He snubbed out the butt of his smoke and got to his feet. Grinning smugly, he hurried to make his preparations.

A bit of an old tune was humming inside his head as he stripped the horses, then led them into the meadow a ways and hobbled them. He wanted them well clear of the camp, and he was sure Vern wouldn't harm them. No, Vern would want the animals himself, to tote the gold on.

The music in his mind stopped as he headed toward the edge of the wood. He was tense and wary as he neared it. Darting in, he grabbed up both hands full of broken branches and hurried back to the sheltering rocks. There, he sorted the sticks and set up for a fire.

Snuffy blinked open his eyes and watched Pike pull the two slicker-wrapped packs of ore together on the ground. He wondered what Pike was up to, poking and prodding at them that way, but he felt too weary to bother asking.

On his knees, Pike measured the bundles with his outstretched arms. End to end, they made a lumpy mound just about the size and shape of a prone man. Careful not to disturb his handiwork, he shoved his saddle up under the far end of one bundle, then spread the blanket over it.

When he stood up and backed off, he was satisfied that by moonlight the mound would look like a man asleep on the ground. Glancing at Snuffy, he wondered if Vern realized a shot had hit the kid. But he wouldn't know how bad the wound was, in any case, would he? And he'd sure be suspicious if it looked like both of them had bedded down.

No, Pike thought, he had to make it look like the kid was on guard. Dropping to a knee, at the boy's side, he said, "Snuffy?"

"Huh?"

"How do you feel?" He tried to sound concerned and sympathetic.

"Not good . . ."

"You've lost a lot of blood. You shouldn't be lying down like that, or you'll lose more."

"Huh?"

He had to convince Snuffy it was important to set up and stay that way. Well, the kid would believe damn near anything he was told.

"Sure. It's like with a canteen. You dump it over on its side with the stopper out, the water all runs out, don't it? You stand it up, the water stays in."

Snuffy pondered that. He hadn't ever thought about it working that way with a hurt man, but it kind of made sense. Leastways, Pike sure sounded like he knew what he was talking about. With effort, the kid moved a hand and tried to raise himself up.

Pike helped. He caught hold of Snuffy's shoulders. It hurt something awful as Pike dragged him to a boulder and propped his back against it. He whimpered at the pain, but he kept himself from complaining. After all, Pike was helping him, and he knew he needed help.

"Now you stay up that way," Pike said, straightening up. He took a few steps back and surveyed his camp. From a distance, it would look like Snuffy was on guard. He just hoped the fool kid didn't pass out and topple over.

With his preparations completed, he finally lit the decoy fire. The smell of woodsmoke should guide Vern right up here, he thought as he clambered into the rocks.

From the perch he chose, he could look down at the mock camp and out across a broad swath of open meadow. Assured that nobody could move in on the camp from the wood, without his spotting him, he drew his gun, punched out the empty cartridges and replaced them. Then he stretched out on his belly to wait.

He sure hoped Vern didn't take too long walking into the trap. Now that the hurrying was done, and he was lying still, he was beginning to feel the weariness in his bones.

Down below, he saw Snuffy's head lean forward, the chin resting on the chest. The kid looked like he'd fallen asleep. Had he passed out or died, Pike wondered. Well, as long as he didn't fall over, it was all right.

The last light of sunset faded. A sky brilliant with stars and a big chunk of ragged-edged moon hung low over Pike's head. At the edge of the forest an owl dropped suddenly to clutch at a scurrying lump of fuzz in the grass. Its claws gripped and its hard bill cracked bone, cutting short the thin squeal of panic.

Pike winced at the sound. Blinking, he realized that he'd dozed off. He squinted through eyelids that felt so heavy he could barely keep them open. With a mumbled curse, he fingered a pinch of tobacco out of the Bull sack and stuffed it into his mouth.

After a few angry chaws at it, he spat on his fingertips and rubbed the stinging tobacco juice into his eyes, then turned his attention to the edge of the woods again.

Dammit, why didn't Vern come?

The two sneak thieves had escaped. They'd jumped onto their horses and disappeared into the woods. As the sounds of their crashing through the brush had faded, the old man had risen to his feet.

Running a hand along the barrel of his rifle, he told himself it was still hexed. That was the only answer. Otherwise at least one of his three shots would have killed. He had a notion he'd hit the young one. He wasn't too sure, though. All the powdersmoke the rifle had kicked back into his face had made it kind of hard to see what went on.

He walked over to the fire the two had left burning and took a deep breath. The chunks of meat hanging over the flame sure smelled good. Real beef meat. That scent roused up a mess of fine memories for him. He recalled a fancy eating place in Denver and a woman with plumes in her hair.

Hunkering, he picked up the spit. There was plenty of time to set and eat. After all, them two had busted a trail through the woods like a berserk grizzly. It'd be easy enough to follow and catch up with them.

The sun was still up over the western peaks when he finished. He paused to kick sand over the embers of the cook fire. This was *his* forest, on *his* mountain, and he sure didn't want any flames running wild through it. Damn fools ought to know better than to go off and leave their fire burning.

He gave the rifle a friendly pat and cradled it under his arm as he started walking again. They knew now that he was on their trail. He figured they'd be on the lookout for him to come sneaking up on their camp tonight. Lot of good it would do them, he thought with a soft chuckle at his own cleverness. Wasn't any pair of claim jumpers going to outfox him on his own mountain. No sir!

CHAPTER
NINE

The sun was still high over the far peaks when Vern squirmed into the hole in the wall of the cave. But no wisp of its light reached into that fissure in the belly of the mountain. Open or closed, his eyes saw nothing. His hands groped ahead of him, feeling out the path through the crawl hole. The rock was knobby and uneven, but not sharp-edged. It felt waterworn, like a crick bottom. This was a kind of underground gully, he thought. And he wondered if there could be flash-floods down here. Lordy, if that was to happen, there sure wouldn't be any way out. There wasn't room enough to turn around, or even to rise up on his hands and knees here. He wriggled, like a snake, and listened apprehensively to that muffled faraway murmur of flowing water. If a sudden flood were to come rushing down this tunnel, he'd hear it all right. He just wouldn't be able to do a damned thing about it.

The crawlway angled, twisting upward and to the side. As he dragged himself into the bend, he caught a sound. Tense, breath caught, he listened.

It was a slow, regular thudding sort of sound, almost like measured footfalls. Lying still, he searched his memory for something similar, but nothing he could recall made a noise like that.

It could be something unknown — something he didn't ever want to know. Or it might be nothing at all worth worrying about. Well, whatever it was, he could keep going and find out, or he could try backing up to the mine again.

To hell with that, he decided. He'd come this far. He'd stick it out. Muttering a hard name at himself, he shoved on.

The tunnel pitched downward again, dropping lower and lower. Its bottom turned to slick mud that had him sliding almost as much as crawling. Then suddenly his searching hands were in icy water.

Slowly, cautious of banging his head, he raised himself up onto his hands and knees. His shoulders brushed stone as cold as ice. Shivering, he moved on. This wasn't any place for a man to be without a shirt. A feller could freeze to death in a spot like this. Damn Pike and Snuffy. He'd sure give them hell . . .

Something tapped him on the back.

He shuddered in stark fear. That couldn't be anything *alive*. Not down here. It had to be the cold ghostly finger of a dead Spaniard that tapped his shoulder blade, hesitated, then tapped again.

He felt it, and he heard the slow measured thudding, close by now. It had a sound like a muffled drum — like a death march — or — dripping water!

His numbing fingers searched along the pool's bottom as he moved on. He sure hoped it didn't get any deeper. Or colder.

It didn't. At last he was out of it, into mud and then onto rock again. The tunnel seemed to go on forever, rising, falling, twisting and turning. Sometimes he had a notion that the roof was far overhead. At other times it scraped his back as he squirmed under it. He felt vagrant air currents from side passages, and his hands warned him of sudden holes. Doggedly, he worked his way past them, following the scent of the man-camp somewhere ahead.

The tunnel stopped. Suddenly, with no warning at all, he found a wall of rock ahead of him. His outstretched fingers traced over it. There was no turning, no trace of a side passage. The tunnel just plain stopped right there. But it couldn't.

Sitting back on his haunches, he stared into the blackness that surrounded him. Had he just crawled all this way into a blind alley — a hole worse than he'd been in back in the mine?

He could still catch the scent of the man-camp in his nostrils, and he could feel the stirring of the air current against his damp shoulders. He told himself that had to be coming from somewhere. The thing to do was *think*. Use his man-sense. Hell, every bit of sense he had told him that camp-smell was coming into this hole from outside. It couldn't come through solid rock, could it?

The air currents twisted and swirled around him. Holding stock still, unbreathing, he tried to judge their touch against his body.

He laughed with relief. No wonder he'd got confused. Up on top of the ground, where a man belonged, the wind hardly ever blew down on a man from straight above. Looking up, into the darkness, he could feel the thin breeze falling directly onto his face.

Kneeling, hands outstretched, he couldn't feel the roof overhead. He unkinked stiff muscles and got to his feet. He still couldn't reach the ceiling. It was like being in the bottom of a well — except that no speck of light showed up above.

There had to be an opening up there somewhere. Maybe another hole and more tunnel before it reached the outside. Whatever it might be, his problem now was to get up there and find it.

His hands found rough outcrops of rock along the wall in front of him. He didn't much like the idea of trying to climb in the dark, with no notion of where he was going or what lay ahead. But there sure didn't seem to be any other way.

Well, with all the scrambling around he'd done out on the face of the mountain, he ought to be getting right good at this rock-climbing business, he told himself. Resigned, he stretched his shoulders, flexed his fingers, and caught a handhold to start hauling himself up.

At first everything was fine. The rough stone gave holds aplenty. But then suddenly the point of rock he'd just grabbed onto came loose in his hand. Off-balance, he felt himself slipping.

Dammit, he didn't want to slide down any more rocks on his belly! Kicking hard at the wall, he jumped away from it.

As his feet touched the ground, he sunk to his knees. Something slammed down onto his shoulder. And something else glanced off the side of his head. He flung his arms up for protection. Rocks were pelting down onto him like a sudden hailstorm. They rained down with a horrible clattering that echoed back and forth, sounding like the whole damned tunnel was caving in.

He huddled against the wall as the rubble hammered on his back. The rumbling thunder of it was like the hoofbeats of a stampeding herd, growing louder and louder. And then, as if the ghostly herd had passed, the thundering began to fade. The shower of stones eased — and was over.

Eyes clenched shut, his arms still wrapped over his head, he listened to the last echoes die away. It hadn't been the whole of the cave that tumbled in on him. There on his knees, he was only thigh-deep in the rubble. The cave was like a feisty bronc, he thought, twisting and snorting and giving him a helluva hard time. But it hadn't throwed him yet. Leastways, he wasn't willing to give up yet.

Drawing a deep breath, he opened his eyes. And saw light.

High above his head, a dim glow broke the pitch-darkness.

He stared at it and choked back the impulse to let out a whoop of joy. That had to be sunlight seeping in. There *was* an opening to the world outside the mountain. He'd won . . .

Well, almost. Now he had to get up there — and to find the hole big enough for a man to squirm through. His heart was banging wildly at his ribs, and his hands trembled as he reached for handholds. He hoped desperately that *all* the loose rock had come tumbling down already. The rest of the wall had to be solid — he hoped.

Slowly, he lifted himself up. Wind gusted through the hole, rich with the scents of the man-camp. His fingers caught at the edge of the opening.

It wasn't very big. He had to stretch both arms out in front of him, digging at stone with his fingers, squirming his body like a snake, to work his way through it. An edge of rock sharp as a knife scraped along his side. He ignored it, dragging himself through.

He was in another chamber of this cave. But this was an open-mouthed one. Beyond the wide gaping hole ahead of him now, there was a sky so brilliant that it almost blinded him.

Stretched out on his belly, motionless, he admired it through thin-slitted eyes. Slowly, his sight adjusted to the light. Not really as brilliant as he'd thought at first, he realized. It was either fair early morning, or late afternoon, depending which direction the cave mouth opened. He breathed deep, thinking it smelled more like afternoon.

There were a lot of scents in the air — the man-camp odor he'd been following was tainted with a smell like fresh meat hanging. That stirred his juices. As he scrambled to his feet, he wondered how long he'd been crawling through the mountain — one day, or two, or for the weeks and weeks that it felt like.

This was the crazy hermit's camp, he thought as he began to examine his surroundings. There was a pallet

124

of dry grass and pelts. Cold ashes in a ring of stones, gear and stores showed that the camp was still in use.

Stepping to the mouth of the cave, he looked out. The old man could be on the way home right now. But scanning the slope down from the cave, he couldn't spot any unnatural motion. And the vast emptiness in his belly was sure raising a complaint. He decided to chance lingering here, hunting out that hanging meat.

It was a fresh quarter of horse, half-hidden in a niche in the wall. As he hauled it into the light, he thought about Red. A damn fine cow-working pony. Too good to go for table meat, but it was too late to do anything about that now.

He shoved a hand into his pocket for the sharp-edged concho. It wasn't much of a knife, but it cut. As he hacked at the meat, he considered the possibility of cooking it. Was it safe to build a fire and wait around here, in the old man's den?

Well, the hermit could be anywhere on the mountain. Wherever he built a fire, its scent might bring the old man sneaking up on him. In here, trouble would have to come through the mouth of the cave. Leastways, nobody could sneak up on him from behind.

Satisfied of that, he collected firewood from the old man's stack against the wall, and built his fire close to the cave's opening, where he could keep watch on the slope below.

While the meat cooked, he ventured to explore the hermit's truck. There were four pouches that felt full of rocks. Gold ore, he thought, not bothering to look into them. Heavy, useless stuff. A man couldn't eat gold. Up here, he couldn't spend it either. And, hell, these pokes surely belonged to the hermit. He didn't want to steal from the old feller.

He left the gold be and went on with his search.

Helping himself to a few provisions didn't seem like stealing. Especially not after the way the old man had taken his horse and gun, and nigh onto killed him. He hoped he'd find the gun somewhere in the cave. But he hadn't any luck. There wasn't a weapon of any kind among the truck. And, aside from the horsemeat, not much food. The airtights would be too hard to open without a knife. But a small sack of parched corn gave him something to nibble at while he waited for the meat to cook. He decided it would be worth taking along when he left. He'd need something to chaw, while he was catching up with Pike and Snuffy.

By the time the meat was ready for eating, the sun had dropped low over the peaks, and it was turning cold up there on the mountain. There was still no sign of the old man coming home for the night, but Vern wanted to be well away from the cave by dark. He kicked out the embers of his fire, then picked up the buffalo robe that lay by the pallet. When he batted it with his hand, dust flew out in a thick cloud. Dirty, and likely full of livestock too. But it would be better than nothing. And it sure did get chilly up here at night. He slung it over his shoulder. Gnawing at the chunk of meat, he headed out of the cave, and across the slope.

As he hunted himself a suitable bedground, he thought about home. And about that load of gold Pike and Snuffy had taken out of the mountain. With his share of that, he'd be going home in style. He sure meant to claim his share. And to give the boys hell for leaving him down in that hole. That was a helluva thing to do to a man. He could have died down there.

He wondered if Pike had *meant* for him to die. It was hard to believe, but yet — he shook his head in discouragement — hell, he couldn't understand Pike at all.

The old man was thinking of home — of his snug cave far up the side of the mountain. He was sure looking forward to finishing off those sneak thieves and getting back to his lair.

As he pushed on through the woods, he thought as how the nights were getting darker than they'd been when he was a young'un. Back then, he could see like a cat. All he needed was a couple of stars, and he could keep going all night. Now, though the sky was wild with pinpoints of light, he couldn't hardly see around him at all. He wondered if the towhead's hex had anything to do with that.

The tang of woodsmoke in the air drew him on and on, until he stumbled over an unseen log. He fell with a jolt that sent a shock of pain through his brittle bones. Sitting up, cursing softly, he gave up. It was just too damned dark.

He knew he was close on to the two sneak thieves. He wanted to catch up with them in their camp tonight. But he couldn't come up on them quietly, if he

127

was going to fall all over the trail. No, he'd have to wait till dawn.

Biting back the impatience in him, he settled on the ground with the rifle in his arms. Tomorrow, he told himself. He'd finish his business with them two tomorrow. He felt real sure of that.

Pike woke suddenly with the overwhelming feeling that something was bad wrong.

Blinking at the pale light of dawn, he knew what was the matter. He'd slept all through the night, and nothing had happened.

A mist hung over the meadow, making the edges of the forest wet blurs. It moistened his face and balled up into dewdrops on his eyelashes. He wiped at it with the back of his hand and looked out from his perch.

The horses were grazing off a ways. Down below, Snuffy lay sprawled on his side, where Pike had left him. He couldn't tell whether the kid was alive or not. Dead, he hoped. He didn't want to be burdened with the damn wounded boy.

The bundled gold lay under the blanket, undisturbed. All around, the grass was frosty with dew that would show clear crisp tracks if anything crossed it. But not a blade seemed out of place.

It was all wrong! Vern was *supposed* to have walked into a trap. Why hadn't it happened? Where was Vern now?

Holding his breath, Pike listened. A silence hung over the meadow, thicker and heavier than the mist. It magnified every faint sound — the shuffling of hooves

128

as one of the horses moved a few steps, the thin trickle of water over rocks, the chirrup of a waking bird. At each small sound, Pike winced.

He was still the quarry, not the hunter. Vern hadn't fallen into his trap. Tense fear surged through him as he thought about it.

He scrambled down the rocks, suddenly damned anxious to be mounted and away from this deathly still meadow.

Snuffy stirred, trying to call to him. The kid's voice came as hoarse as a death rattle. It hit Pike like a spur, jabbing him to move even faster.

He lunged across the meadow, his boots leaving dark smears in the dewy grass. Startled, the horses stared apprehensively at him and shied away as he reached to catch them. He got hold of his own mount and got the bridle onto it. But the bay managed to crow-hop in the hobbles, playing him along until he was sweating and cursing. When he finally got the reins looped over its neck, it made him fight to get the bit between its clenched teeth.

He was burning with anger by the time he led the two animals back to the campsite. When Snuffy tried speaking to him, he spat a hard name at the kid and went on with the work of saddling the horses and loading up the bundles of ore.

He was still mumbling curses when he finished that chore and turned toward Snuffy. From the look of him, the kid would probably have to be tied to his saddle. Probably be hollering to rest all day long, Pike thought resentfully as he held out a hand toward the kid.

Something snapped past his head. The morning stillness was shattered by the blast of a rifle.

Pike wheeled, his fingers groping for the pistol at his side. Through the mist, he spotted a dark figure at the wood's edge.

"Vern!" he grunted, his voice thin with fear.

The bay reared. Snorting, it bolted. For an instant Pike stared at it as it lunged across the meadow. Half of his gold was packed on that animal!

His own mount was dancing its forehooves, uncertain whether to obey the dragging reins, or to light out after its panicked companion.

Pike grabbed for those trailing reins with one hand. The other had found the Colt. Waving it, he clawed back the hammer and let it slip. The wild shot snapped like a crack of thunder.

As he slung himself up onto the saddle, he could see that shadowy figure, through the mists fumbling with the rifle.

Jammed, he thought with a surge of hopeful excitement. Grabbing breath, he held rein on the horse and steadied himself. Sketching out his arm, he sighted along the top strap of the pistol. It wavered nervously. He slapped the other hand up under his, bracing it. And fired.

The dark figure winced. Hit!

As Pike jabbed spurs into his mount's sides, he saw the sniper's rifle flash harsh orange and heard the boom of it. But it was downtilted, slamming its lead into the grass. The man holding it was slumping into a small heap.

130

"Pike?" Snuffy called.

But Pike didn't look back. He'd stopped that damned killer who'd been tracking him. Now his attention was all on the dark streak the runaway horse's hooves had scraped through the misted grass. He had to catch the bay with the treasure loaded on it.

Struggling, Snuffy got himself up onto his elbows. His head was light, giddy-feeling inside, but his body was like a lead weight. It took all his strength to prop it up. He squinted at the blurred figure of the rider disappearing into the fog, then looked toward that crumpled figure lying at the edge of the forest.

"Vern?" he called hoarsely. "Vern!"

There was no response.

Snuffy eased his head down again. He lay there on the damp earth with tears burning in his eyes. Everything in the world had gone wrong. Pike had shot Vern and had run off. Now Vern was dead. And he had an awful strong feeling that he was dying himself.

He didn't care what the hell Pike said. It wasn't right! Not none of it!

CHAPTER
TEN

The night had been cold, but as the day grew, the sun pounded its heat down onto the open expanses dotting the slopes. Crossing them, Vern felt it burning against his bare shoulders. His skin was already sore. Now it was beginning to itch and peel. And he was mad.

As he scrambled downward, he rehearsed the cussing out he intended to give Pike and Snuffy once he caught up with them. He planned to give Pike more than just one piece of his mind. Hell of a thing to go off and leave a man down in a hole that way. Pike deserved a good thrashing for that.

Maybe he deserved more than just a thrashing. Vern knew some folk would figure he deserved a dose of lead. But Vern had never felt much inclination to use his gun on anything but varmints. Gunplay could get awful final. He didn't really want to kill anybody — not even Pike.

No, he'd settle his debt to Pike with his fists and claim his share of that gold. Then everything would be squared up and they could all have a few drinks together and be friends again.

Passing from the open slope into a shadowed woods was like crawling out of a fire. As soon as the sun was no longer beating directly down on him, Vern felt better. When he came onto the path the two horses had broken through the underbrush, he began to feel just fine again. He figured he couldn't be far behind the pair of them now. He'd catch up soon and it'd be a real fine thing to hear a human voice again.

Sure couldn't be far behind them, he thought as he ambled through the brush. There was a smell of fresh horse droppings not too far away.

And more than just that! He stopped suddenly as a suggestion of rancid tallow and stale sweat tingled in his nostrils. Vivid images jumped into his mind — recollections of being lashed down with wet rawhide, of having a gun-barrel poked into his backbone, of running like hell to escape a crazy old man who'd wanted to kill him.

Moving with quiet caution, he approached the edge of the woods. One hand was thrust into his pocket, wrapped tight around that lucky Jackson cent. Luck was a mighty fickle friend. His had sure got strung out thin in spots lately. He hoped desperately that it wouldn't break on him now. If that crazy hermit was lying in wait out there . . .

Something rumpled the tall grass just beyond the trees. Something that looked awful like a dead man. Pausing, Vern stared at it. He recognized the old man's fringed jacket. Dead? From the way he was lying, he looked it.

Vern walked toward him slowly. Then he saw the flies and heard their scornful buzzing. The old feller was dead, all right.

Hunkering, he prodded a finger at the buckskin-covered shoulder. His hands didn't want anything to do with a corpse. But a person couldn't just up and ignore a dead man. Not even a crazy old hermit who'd meant to kill him. Death was an awesome thing. A feller couldn't help but feel respectful toward the dead.

His hands gently turned the body. Open eyes gazed blindly toward the midday sun. The mouth gaped, lips drawn back from rotten stumps of teeth, tight with the stiffness that came to cold flesh. A beetle scurried out of the matted beard, hurrying along the front of the jacket, heedless of the dry brown stains it crossed.

The bloodstain surrounded a big ragged wound. A forty-five, Vern figured. Pike's or Snuffy's most likely. To judge from the way the fired-off rifle lay at the old man's fingertips, he'd been shooting back.

A vague sense of sympathy and guilt stirred in Vern. These mountains were an alien place to him, but the old man had belonged up here. He'd been trying to drive intruders out of his domain. A man couldn't rightly hold him to blame for that. No, it was he — Vern — along with Pike and Snuffy, who'd been in the wrong. They'd stayed up here, hunting and taking gold they didn't really have any right to. Now, because of that the old man was dead.

Vern told himself he should have stuck to the job of hunting the strayed beefs. Should have tried harder to talk Pike and Snuffy into sticking to it, too. But it was too late to worry over that now. Best he could do to make amends would be to pile some *rocks* over the body. Keep the varmints from getting at it. Sighing, he started to his feet.

Something called his name.

Instinctively, he scooped up the old man's rifle. But that hadn't sounded like anything a gun would stop. It had a whispery, wind-thin sound that rattled like death. For an instant he was certain clear through to his bones that it was the ghost of the hermit, come to pay him back for wanting to steal that Spanish gold.

But when the call came again, there was something awful familiar in it.

"Snuffy?"

"Help me, Vern."

He found the kid lying by the rocks, trying futilely to sit up. Dropping to his knees at the boy's side, he let the rifle slide out of his hand. "Snuff! What's happened?"

"Hurt," the kid mumbled. His groping fingers reached toward Vern. They caught his outstretched hand. With shuddering effort, the boy lifted his head off the ground.

Vern saw the smears of blood covering his shirtfront. He whispered, "Hold on, Snuff. Take it easy."

"Don't hurt me again, Vern. Don't — don't shoot me no more."

"Huh!"

"Please don't . . ." Snuffy's fingers dug sharply into his arm, then eased off as the kid ran out of strength. The hand slipped away and the boy's eyes closed.

"Snuffy!" Vern said, staring incredulously at the kid. How could Snuffy think *he* had fired that shot?

The lump in the kid's chaps pocket was the bandanna-wrapped ore they'd first found. Vern jerked it out, dumping the gold on the ground, and headed for water. He brought back the dampened scarf and wiped at the kid's face with it.

The carrot-colored lashes flickered, then parted. In a faint, rasping voice, Snuffy repeated, "Please don't hurt me again. Please."

"*I* didn't do it! *I* wouldn't hurt you, Snuff. You know that."

"Not you?"

"*No!*"

"But — but you've come for me, ain't you? You're dead and now I'm dead too and you come for me . . ."

"Ain't neither of us dead." Vern fingered open the boy's shirt and carefully peeled the cloth back from the wound. The bullethole was pinched up under a thick scab of blood. Even so, it looked bad. Festering, Vern thought. Seemed like nothing at all had been done for it, not even a wad of cloth stuffed over it to stay the bleeding.

"What happened?" he asked dully. He had a damned bitter helpless feeling that it was too late for Snuffy. The wound had been left untended too long and had spilled out too much blood. There wasn't anything much that could be done now, except to comfort the kid as best he could, and see that he got decent buried.

"Shot. Bushwhacked," Snuffy mumbled. "Pike said it was you."

"No! It was that old hermit I told you about."

"Hermit? Was there really a hermit, Vern?"

He nodded in reply. "But he's dead now. Wasn't it *you* that shot *him*?"

"Pike. He shot — said it was you. Where is he, Vern? Why don't he come back for me?"

Glancing around, he asked, "Where'd he go? When?"

"This mornin', sunrise — shot you and rode off." Snuffy's eyes closed again. Behind the scattering of freckles, his face was pale as bleached bone. The gaunted flesh lay taut over his skull. He was damn close to dead, Vern thought. Where the hell had Pike gone? How could he have left Snuffy lie here all morning like this? How could he have left him at all?

Vern wiped the damp scarf over the kid's face again as he pieced together what must have happened. He would work out the *how* of it, but not the *why*. There couldn't be any reason in the world why Pike would have gone off and left Snuffy alone here to die. It just plain didn't make any sense at all

The bay horse was carrying a load of ore, but it wasn't burdened with the weight of a rider as well. It led Pike on one devil of a chase before he could catch more than just a glimpse of it scooting through the rocks. But when it burst into the open, zigzagging across a high barren, he finally gained ground. Closing on the bay, he swung his rope. It was a good throw. When the bay felt the tug of the rope, tied hard, it gave up the fight.

Pike slid out of the saddle, took a couple of strides to stretch his legs, and sat down on a rock. As he built himself a smoke, he looked back the way he'd come in chase of the bay. He'd rode a fair piece. Seemed like a damned waste of time to have to go all the way back for Snuffy. Besides that, it'd keep slowing him down, having to haul a cripple along. Might even keep him from getting to Cheyenne ahead of the herd. Then there'd be the danger of running into the Boss or some of the trail hands before he could get onto a train heading west. Dammit, why the hell did the kid have to go and get himself shot up like that?

Snuffy'd probably die from the wound, he told himself. Maybe he was dead already.

He thought about the waste it would be if he backtracked and then found a cold corpse. Flinging away the butt of the cigarette, he mumbled, "The hell with it!"

There wasn't any sense at all in burdening himself with a dying man. No sense in loading the horses with unnecessary weight. Smart thing to do would be put the whole load of ore onto Snuffy's bay and keep heading north from here.

Hell it was the fool kid's own fault for getting shot up that way, he thought as he began to pull the makeshift pack off his mount. Snuffy didn't deserve being bothered with. Probably dead by now anyway.

Once he had the bundle secured on the bay's saddle, he collected reins and swung up onto his own horse. Whistling softly, cheerfully, he contemplated the good times all that gold would buy.

He was feeling right pleased with himself. This time he was sure Vern was dead. Shot him down himself, hadn't he? A steady hand on a Colt forty-five was all a man needed to get what he wanted in this world.

It occurred to him he was beginning to want something to fill the empty spot in his belly. Well, a forty-five would get him that, too. He slowed the pace to an easy amble, watching the land for sign of game.

It was somewhere after noon when he spotted deer sign. It was right fresh. Grinning to himself, he urged his horse up the trail it indicated.

He spotted the young doe at a waterhole, head down, unaware of him. His first shot caught it in the flank, sending it plunging toward the woods in an awkward, frantic limp. The second shot wasn't so good. But the third one struck meat.

The doe staggered, fell, and struggled to its feet again. Blood was spurting from its side. Its haunches trembled, then collapsed. Its head held high, it tried desperately to drag itself along with its forehooves.

Pike holstered the gun. He only had a few rounds left. No point in wasting them, he figured. Dismounting, he headed for the deer.

It stared at him, shuddering with pain and panic. He nudged it with his toe. It winced. Real fine piece of eating, he thought, licking at his lips in anticipation. Drawing his sheath knife, he grabbed at its neck.

Hot blood spewed onto his hand as he slashed into the animal's throat. It gave one final convulsive shudder. Then it went limp.

Somewhere within the woods a cat screamed.

Pike jerked up his head, scanning the shadows under the trees. He didn't like that at all. The blood scent would bring the panther to investigate. Even though he had a gun in his hand, he didn't fancy tangling with a cat. No, he'd pack up his kill and get the hell out of here. Build his fire and make his camp somewhere in the clear, where a cat couldn't sneak up unseen.

The bay shied as he hefted the doe's body, trying to heave it across the saddle. Cursing, he slapped at the horse's face with a rein end. It shied again, ducking back, and the heavy weight of the deer slipped out of his grip. The smell of fresh blood had the nervous bay bad upset. Disgusted, Pike turned instead to his own horse. It was better-trained. It didn't give him so much fight. He got the carcass tied behind his saddle and mounted up, eager to get moving before that cat showed up.

It took a long piece of riding and searching, but he finally found a campsite that suited him just fine. Ragged upthrusts of rock gave way to a shallow slope that ended abruptly against the sky. There were clumps of grass the horses could nibble, and a few gnarled bushes that could be broken up for firewood. The wind blew in fierce gusts over the rim of the cliff, but a cluster of boulders offered windbreak enough for the fire.

Swinging off his horse, he ambled over to the edge of the cliff and looked down curiously. One quick glance was enough. He backed away from the edge hurriedly. The drop-off was sudden and sharp, straight down. Far below, a jumble of sharp, jagged stones upthrust from the shadows. Just looking down that way gave him a dropping feeling in the pit of his stomach.

With a good span of land between himself and the brink, he looked across toward the valley. The twilight

140

shadows and evening mist had begun to form down there, but he could still see a dark blur that must be the herd.

He grinned at the thought of all the fool drovers out there eating dust in the drag and wearing their butts to the bone for a few dollars, while here *he* was on top of the world. A whole horseload of ore, almost pure gold, and it was his — *all* his! There was nobody left alive who could claim any part of it from him.

Turning back to the horses, he pulled down the deer's carcass. Once he stripped the saddles and had the horses' hobbled, he set in to butchering. By the time that was done and the meat was over his fire, twilight had reached up here, onto the high places. The rising wind made a long, lonely wailing over the edge of the cliff. But the glow of the fire was real warm and friendly against the night chill. When he heard the cry of a cat again, it came from far away.

With his belly full and a saddle blanket wrapped over his shoulders, Pike felt content. At peace with the world.

The sunlight was dying fast, setting on a cold and ugly world, as Vern hunkered to examine fresh bloodstains on the earth. A deer, he thought. There were cat tracks, and the marks of claws digging into the bloody ground, but he felt sure it wasn't a panther that had made the kill. No, he was pretty sure that deer had been shot.

Straightening up, clutching the ancient trade rifle, he moved on along the trace the horse's hooves had made. It was getting dark fast. Be too dark for tracking before long. He glanced at the shadowed woods around him, hating it. This ragged land with its spook-ridden forests and the thin, strange-smelling air, was unnatural. Not country meant for man.

A man left home trailing cattle so he could make a little money and see something of the world. When he did it, he knew he might end up with his bones heaped in some alien place. There were plenty of ways of getting killed on the trail. A man could take a bad fall off a randy bronc or go down under the hooves of the running herd. He might be hooked by an ornery ladino, or even get attacked by renegades off their reservation. He knew about things like that when he signed on, and he could be ready in his mind to face them. It was all part of the job.

But the way Snuffy had died — that wasn't part of anything. It was useless. Shot down by a crazy old man, then abandoned by a *friend*. Pike's trail had proven he'd never tried to go back after the boy. He'd just plain run out and abandoned him. Why? For a load of damned yellow metal? Was *that* worth the kid's life?

If the wound had been tended immediately — if Snuffy had been taken straight to the trail crew for help — he might have pulled through. It had damned well been Pike's *duty* to take care of him and get him help. But Pike had run out. Now Snuffy's body lay under a pile of rocks on the side of a mountain a hell of a long way from his own land, with no marker but the kid's empty hand gun.

A cat, like the one that howled in the distance, killed for food. A rattler killed to protect itself. Yet men

142

destroyed them both on sight. Pike had killed for gold. He was less than a man — less than a cat or a rattler. To Vern's mind, he was less than any varmint that roamed the plains.

Pike would never live to spend Snuffy's share of that Spanish treasure. That was one thing Vern was damned sure of. He'd see to it, even if it cost him his own life.

CHAPTER
ELEVEN

An unfamiliar impatience rankled Vern as he settled for the night. He wasn't used to lying awake, once he'd bedded down. Or to worrying much at all. But the urge to get caught up to Pike was a strong hard spur. It kept thoughts racing through his head as he lay there gazing at a dark jut of cliff silhouetted against the star-flecked sky.

He wasn't aware of falling asleep, but only of waking suddenly with the thought sharp in his mind that he had to get moving, and get this business done with. But it was too early yet. The colors of dawn were just beginning to smear across the morning sky. It wasn't light enough to see the sign the horses had left in the woods.

But he was too anxious to sleep any more. So he sat huddled against the lingering chill, waiting, wondering. An orange star blinked, catching his attention. It seemed to sit right on the edge of that outjutting cliff, and to flicker as he watched.

It blinked again. Something, or someone, had moved in front of it, Vern thought as he scrambled to his feet. It wasn't any star. That was a campfire burning up

144

there on the ledge. Hurrying as fast as he could in the darkness, he headed toward it.

The sky brightened, and the sun slowly poked an edge over the far peaks, looking as if it had set blaze to the rim of the world. It cast long shadows into the jumble of massive rocks that lay between Vern and the cliff. He threaded among them, the long rifle clutched in his hand. As he reached their far edge, he stopped suddenly, catching his breath and holding it. He'd glimpsed a horse.

Working his way cautiously, he approached the open slope. His heart was banging in his chest, his lungs were cramped with excitement as he halted in the shadows, to scan the slope.

The horses were saddled and loaded, standing ground-hitched in the scant grass. A ways beyond them, a thin twist of smoke rose from behind a cluster of boulders. Wind rising over the brink of the cliff caught the smoke, scattering it, filling the air with the scent of burning wood and cooking meat.

A long shadow stretched out from the boulders. It moved. The rocks didn't.

Watching it, Vern judged a man to be sitting behind those rocks, resting his back against them, and eating.

The ancient trade rifle was already loaded. Vern had seen to that before he'd left Snuffy's grave. But he didn't trust flintlocks. Just to be sure, he lifted the frizzen and renewed the primer charge, then closed it again with silent caution. But he couldn't muffle the sharp click as he dragged the heavy hammer back to full cock.

The horses looked toward him, their heads high and their eyes wary. Evidentally Pike hadn't heard it, though. The shadow didn't move.

Vern hesitated, thinking maybe he should wait until Pike finished eating and came out to collect the animals. But if the horses kept watching him that way, Pike would notice and get suspicious. No, he couldn't chance the nervous, curious horses betraying his presence. He had to act now.

Slowly, tensely, he slid out of the gap between the rocks. The horses stared at him as he walked into the open. He had to angle and swing around the boulders that shielded Pike. But he couldn't come up on him from the west. That would put the blinding fire of the sun behind Pike, full into his own eyes. Instead, he moved eastward, toward the rim of the cliff.

He glanced down. A helluva long drop. Edging away from the brink a bit, he took another step forward. And glimpsed the fire. Dropping to his belly, with the rifle across his arms, he squirmed forward another few feet.

Now he could see Pike sitting there, nibbling meat off the spit. Pike looked completely at ease and off guard. It should be a real easy shot.

Vern knew that prone, with the brilliance of the sun behind his own back, he wasn't likely to catch Pike's attention. But still there was a knot of nervousness twisting in his gut as he lifted himself to his elbows. Behind him, the horses stared and snuffled, sensing his tension.

He raised the gun, snugging the butt against his shoulder. The muzzle was heavy, the old weapon an

146

unfamiliar thing that wavered in his hands. Steadying it, he gazed down the barrel. With precise care, he set the sights square in line with Pike's body.

Pike turned his head, a vague and uncertain puzzlement on his face as he squinted toward the sun.

Vern closed his finger on the trigger.

The hammer slapped down, flint slamming sparks against the frizzen. In the pan, powder sputtered and flared through the firehole. The big rifle bucked hard as it spat lead. White smoke whipped from the pan and muzzle, the blast booming in Vern's ears. The wind flung the smoke back, stinging, into his eyes.

Blinking, he saw chips of rock fly from the boulder a good couple of handspans from Pike's head. Pike was leaping up, grappling the revolver from his holster.

Anger and disgust surged through Vern. He'd missed! The damned old rifle wasn't sighted right. It had thrown bad to the left. Now Pike was up — warned — armed.

Vern's hands went for the powder horn and shot pouch. But he knew it was no use. He couldn't lie here and get the single-shot rifle reloaded in time. Rolling, clinging to the gun, he scrambled up and ran. If he could get back to the jumble of rocks — take cover there and reload — maybe —

The bay snorted, white-rimmed eyes staring at the man plunging toward it. Nerves frayed by the past days, it reared to strike out at the charging threat.

Vern saw the horse go up. He knew it meant to smash those iron-shod forehooves down on him. He swerved.

Pike's gun cracked out its thunder.

The bay snorted. Its hooves struck earth. It lunged forward, foam flagging from its open mouth. The flapping off-stirrup grazed Vern's arm. The animal leaped past him. Suddenly, in mid-stride, its forelegs folded. Heaving, it toppled. He glimpsed the blood spurting from its side, saw it raise its head, tossing in agony. Then, with a shudder, it sank to the ground.

Pike's second shot lashed at the earth, flinging up shards of rubble inches ahead of Vern. He caught himself, balanced for an instant, knowing he'd never make it to the rocks alive.

Wheeling around, he jumped. And sprawled face down beside the fallen horse.

The other horse — Pike's own mount — snorted at the stench of hot blood. With a frenzied whinny, it bolted. It ran straight toward Pike. Vern saw him duck, then leap to grab at the reins.

The horse would hold Pike's attention for a moment, maybe longer. Maybe long enough —

Vern dragged the muzzle of the rifle across his chest. His hand trembled as he dumped powder into the bore. There was blood on his fingers — slick wet blood that had spattered him as he dropped beside the dying horse. The rifle ball slipped out of his grip. It was lost in the rubble.

As he groped into the shot pouch for another, he heard Pike fire again.

The slicker-wrapped bundle lashed to the bay's saddle was inches from Vern's face. It jerked as lead slammed into it, puffing dust into his eyes. He

148

squirmed, pressing himself close against the horse's carcass for cover. But how much good was that cover when Pike had a loaded gun, and he didn't?

The thoughts were racing wild through his mind. He had a sick feeling he'd never get the damned flintlock loaded again. Not unless he could somehow grab a whole hunk of time to do it in.

But Pike had spent three shots already. At most he only had three left in the revolver. Then *he'd* have to pause to reload.

Three shots left. But *one* would be enough, if Pike could put it in the right place, Vern thought bitterly. How the devil could he sucker Pike into missing three more times?

Cautiously he edged up his head. He saw Pike clinging to the panicked horse, his left hand up close to the bit. With his right, he was leveling the Colt.

Vern jerked back as lead snarled close past his face. The fourth shot — but too damned close. Poking his head up was a helluva way to draw fire. Especially when Pike was so close. Unless he could get Pike too excited to shoot straight at all.

Hugged up against the carcass of the horse, he caught hold of one of the saddle strings and jerked. The knot slid apart. The slicker gaped open, spilling a heavy sack and loose chunks of ore.

Grabbing the sack, Vern lifted it up and shouted, "Pike! Gold!"

He flung the poke with as much strength as he could from his awkward position. It soared out, over the rim of the cliff, and disappeared.

Pike's scream was a wild, animal cry that tore from deep within his throat. His shot drowned it out. The slug thonked into the body of the dead horse.

Just once more! Vern grabbed another poke from the slicker and sent it sailing out over the edge of the cliff. As he jerked back his hand, pain screamed through his arm. A red streak appeared suddenly, cutting across his flesh halfway between wrist and elbow. It burned as if a hot branding iron had been laid against his skin.

That shoot had been *too* close, he thought as he leaped to his feet. Too close — but it had been the sixth shot.

As he lunged from cover of the carcass, he saw Pike running toward him, waving the Colt.

Vern's sudden appearance startled Pike. Swinging the gun toward his bold target, he jerked the trigger.

There was no answering thunder — no hard buck of the Colt against his palm. The firing pin snapped against an empty casing. The lack he'd been braced for didn't come. Off-balance in mid-stride, he lurched forward.

Vern heard the futile click of the hammer. Wheeling, he saw Pike going down onto his hands and knees, the gun sliding from his grip.

Grabbing the weapon up again, Pike scrambled to his feet. Instinctively, he clawed back the hammer. But he realized the gun was empty. And Vern was charging *toward* him now. He jerked it up, meaning to smash out with it like a club.

Vern lunged toward Pike, intending to grapple — to fight. But the sudden upjerk of Pike's hand gave him an

150

instant of warning. He twisted to the side as the gun-weighted hand slammed down toward his head. The knuckles grazed his cheek, the blow glancing against his shoulder.

He swung himself past Pike's left side, spinning around. His outflung arm hooked Pike's neck. Startled, Pike fell back against him. The man's weight ramming into him sent him sprawling back. He dragged Pike down with him.

Arms flailing, Pike broke loose of his grip and rolled. He grabbed out, fingers clawing at Pike's shirt. Tugging free, Pike jerked himself up onto his knees.

Pike had dropped the gun. But his bony fist was clenched into a hard knot as it plunged toward Vern's face.

Vern jerked back, trying to squirm away. The knuckles slammed into his cheek. Flinging up an arm, he grabbed for Pike's wrist.

As Pike wrenched against Vern's thumb, breaking the grip, Vern flung up his other hand. It caught Pike just under the breastbone. It was an awkward blow, without much force, but it dragged a sharp grunt of surprise out of Pike. He rocked back on his haunches.

Vern rolled, coming up onto his own knees, throwing both fists toward Pike's belly. Pike fended one. The other found soft flesh and sunk deep into it.

Groaning, Pike hugged his arms against his body and bent forward. He doubled over, face down, and lay still.

Vern dragged a deep, relieved breath and got slowly to his feet. He glanced around for the revolver, spotted

151

it and started to turn toward it. Pike's arm shot out, wrapping around his ankles, jerking hard.

Vern went down — flat on his back. Pike flung himself across him, swinging astride his thighs to hammer fists at his gut.

Vern felt the sharp edge of rock under his shoulders. And nothing at all under his head. The wind whipped up the face of the cliff, lapping around his cheeks like the heavy shocks of pain into his belly.

He twisted, trying to buck, trying to squirm away from Pike's assault — and from the edge of the cliff. Flinging up his hands, he caught at Pike's shirt. Cloth tore under his fingers.

As he rammed his fists into Vern's body, Pike at first saw only the blurred figure he straddled. He blinked, wanting to clear his vision — wanting to see Vern's face.

He saw it. And beyond it, he saw the vast expanse of space past the brink of the cliff.

Fear clutched his gut, knotting it. He jerked back, suddenly more afraid of that drop than of Vern. Wildly, he flung himself back. He ran.

Vern felt the weight that had pinned him suddenly gone. Rolling, he dragged himself away from the brink and rose up onto his arms. Pain filled his belly, flooding up into his chest, burning in his throat and blurring in his eyes.

He glimpsed Pike scurrying away, then pausing to look back.

Safe strides away from the edge of the cliff, Pike felt that surge of panic fade. He looked at Vern sprawled on the ground, seeming too badly beaten to stand up. And

152

there was only one thought in his mind — he had to kill Vern. Now!

He scanned the ground for some weapon, and saw the trade rifle lying by the carcass of the horse. It was empty, but it would make a hefty club. One that could crush a man's skull with a single blow — Vern's skull.

Vern lay motionless, watching through slitted eyes. The pain that began in his belly muscle stretched itself through his whole body. He wasn't sure he could stand up if he tried. He knew he couldn't run fast or far if he did make it to his feet.

He saw Pike bend and rise again with the heavy weapon in his hands. He'd grabbed it by the barrel and swung it up over his shoulder. Gravel crunched under his boots as he started toward Vern.

Even the gusting winds seemed to pause in tense anticipation. Their moaning faded until there was no sound but Pike's steps.

Vern knew what Pike intended to do with the gun. And he knew he couldn't just lie there and be murdered. Cautiously he drew one arm back a fraction of an inch, shifting his weight, bracing himself.

Pike's lips drew back from his teeth in a death's-head grin. The heart was banging wildly in his chest. His hands trembled with excitement. A moment more and it would be done. Eagerly, he hefted the rifle and lunged toward Vern, swinging it.

With a shove of his arm, Vern rolled.

His shoulder slammed against Pike's leg. He felt Pike's other foot, raised in mid-stride, ram into his ribs.

Pike squealed in surprise as he stumbled. The gun swinging in his hands was a heavy weight. Its momentum twisted him. He turned in a full circle, trying to recover his balance. His feet shuffled in an awkward backstep.

Vern saw Pike's boot touch the brink of the cliff. Pushing himself up onto his arms, he shouted. But it was too late.

He saw Pike turning again, facing outward into the sky, a stick-figure silhouetted against the golden fire of the morning sun.

Pike disappeared as suddenly as if that blaze had consumed him. But his shrieking wail was a long moment dying.

The wind that curled up over the rim of the cliff whispered a mockery of the scream.

Vern closed his eyes and drew a deep breath, trying to calm the sudden shivering that ran through his marrow. When he opened them again, the sun was still a burning disc atop a distant peak. The wind still made its mocking murmur along the ledge.

He dragged himself to his feet and walked into that wind. Still with the shuddery feeling along his spine, he peered over the brink. The jumbled rocks were far below. Only their highest points rose from the shadows to catch the sun's light. Something on one of them sparkled. Just a pinpoint of light. Maybe gold, he thought. Maybe not.

He wiped at his face with the back of one hand. Despite the chill winds, he was covered with sweat. And weary. Suddenly he was just too damned tired and aching to stand up. Lowering himself stiffly, he stretched out on the ground and pressed his face into the crook of his arm.

When he opened his eyes again, the sun was high. Its heat was baking into his bare back. With a grunt he sat up and looked around.

Pike's horse had drifted back a ways. It stood off across the slope, cropping *grass* as peacefully as a yoke ox. Watching it, he thought that he wouldn't have much trouble catching it, if he moved in slow and easy. He could ride back here to collect those pokes of gold and then . . .

Then what? That damned gold had already caused him a lot of aches and pains. It had cost him his clothes, his gun and his horse. Well, once he got it into a town it'd buy him new ones and a lot more besides.

But it was a dead man's gold and it had already killed. It had cost Pike and Snuffy and the old hermit their lives, as well as the Spaniards who'd first mined it. And it had come too close to killing him a couple or three times, too.

He walked over to the carcass of the bay. Flies buzzed angrily at him as he picked up one of the pokes. He let ore trickle into his palm. It caught sunlight, like little flames dancing in his palm.

Dead man's gold, with no luck in it but the bad kind, he told himself as he tossed it into the wind. The tiny sparks flickered and died in the shadows at the foot of the cliff.

The slicker-wrapped bundle was a heavy load to drag to the brink. When he kicked it over more of the pokes opened to spatter moments of flashing gold into the sunlight. It showered down and disappeared.

He heaved the second bundle after it.

One chunk of ore still lay on the ledge. It was almost pure metal, with just bits of white rock clinging to it. As he picked it up, he felt an urge to shove just this one piece into his pocket. Just enough to buy him a new shirt, a gun and a horse . . .

He turned it, catching light on its *shining* face. And he saw the splotch of dried blood. Probably the horse's blood. But it might well have been Snuffy's. Or his own. It didn't take a very big piece of bad-luck gold to kill a man.

Pike had wanted the damned stuff bad enough to do murder for it. Let him have it *all*. He flung the shard into the sky and turned his back.

Nobody got something for nothing, he thought as he walked toward the grazing horse. A man paid for everything — if not in work, then in trouble or maybe in his own blood.

He wondered what chance he'd have of locating that old golondrino and the rest of the strays. Where they'd been they'd had plenty of graze and water. Shouldn't have drifted far. If he could get them bunched, he was certain he could drive them on up to the herd all right. And it might help smooth things over when he got back to the herd if he'd finished the job he'd been sent to do.

Glancing at his tattered britches and makeshift moccasins, he owned to himself that likely he was going to have a hell of a time explaining to the Boss what had happened.

156